CONVERSATIONS OF **MEN**

SPENCER KELLY

authorHOUSE®

AuthorHouse™
1663 Liberty Drive
Bloomington, IN 47403
www.authorhouse.com
Phone: 833-262-8899

Published by AuthorHouse 03/24/2022

ISBN: 978-1-6655-5586-9 (sc)
ISBN: 978-1-6655-5585-2 (e)

Library of Congress Control Number: 2022905619

CONTENTS

INTRODUCTION

Conversation of men is a book about four best friends who lives changed over the years. They share their ups and downs with each other and what their friendship has endured through the years, but people change and emotions too. After seven years of incarceration in prison Mike tries to understand but are the guys ready for Mike's new changes? When Mike left the streets, Omar was just marrying Tosha who was pregnant with his second baby, Tony was still trying to become the next Johnnie Cochran, while Louis was just trying to find his place in the world. After being away, Mike has a lot of questions that had been lingering on his mind for the last couple of years ever since that night with Omar. Mike has always wondered what would of happen if things would have been handle different, what would his life be like today. For the next few months, the guys will put everything on the table. The conversations these guys will have amongst each other will answer a lot of questions that need to be answered. All the doubts and regrets will be brought to the surface. Old memories of past relationships, arguments and disagreements will emerge. Will the pack they made as young men be strong enough to weather the storm that lies ahead? Will Omar life be turned upside down again? Will past love choices in life catch up with him? Will Tony's surprise arrival make him become the man that he's capable of being? Can these four men handle the conversations of their lives?

CHAPTER ONE

(MIKE)

Mike laid in the bed looking up into space, remembering all he has been through and all the losses he took the past seven years, but also thinking about all the knowledge that he had gain while in prison. The first couple of years was a blur to Mike, because everybody was always there to take care of his needs, but after people started slacking and not being there, that's when shit started to change, and he felt like his sentence really began and having time to understand the things that is happening around him. Sometimes the walls inside the jail can play mind games on you. My boys stayed down the whole time, visiting me and making sure that I had anything I needed. I told myself that I wouldn't bother them as much, because I didn't want to be a burden to them, but every time I looked around, there they were. Don't get me wrong, it was nice having them there, but somethings you want to do yourself. My mom and dad died my first couple of years in here, and I've refused to attend the funeral, but my boys went and kind of felt like they were representing me too. I was an only child with plenty open my eyes to a lot of things. Didn't really know what my purpose on earth was until he enlightened me. All through life we seem to be trying to fit into places that's not for us, and in relationships that not good or healthy for us. Our parents use to try and tell us but, we were too caught up in our own lives, trying to figure things out on our own. But life has a funny way of showing you, that you're not in control sometimes. Never really prayed until I meet Mr. Rod, didn't really understand the bible, who God was or nothing, so trying to understand and believe in God, was a little bit hard at first. Going to church in prison was a little strange at first, because these men was praising God, crying real tears and nothing was wrong with them. I believe in God now and I'm trying to understand God's plans for me, back then I was wild and crazy, and out of control. Quick to do everything, not a care in the world. Now things have really change, there's something inside of me that doesn't allow me to be wild and crazy anymore. My biggest concern now is will the guys be able to handle and understand the new me, Mr. Rod said if they're my real friends that they will understand me.

Hundreds of relatives all over, but I never seen one while I was in prison, not a single letter, until the week before my release. The money that I gotten from my mom's and dad insurance was invested in all kinds of things by Omar. When I was packing my things, a picture drops out of my bag of me and the boys. It was a photo we had taken before all the madness happen. Back then there was no wives, or children, just us fellows doing our thing and whatever that was. I guess you can say time and life has changed us all. My cell mate asked me what the first thing was I was going to do when I left this place, things were moving so fast that I really haven't given that much thought. Listening to some of the things that they planned and said they would do was far from my mind, I had lost a lot of things while I was locked up, things I couldn't get back. Spending a lot of time alone has really open my eyes to the things that I took for granted, can't catch up for the time I lost, but I can enjoy the time I have left. Rod was an older Christian man in the joint I met that then suddenly I was shaken out of my thoughts by the guard, telling me to pack my things up, it's time for me to leave.

CHAPTER TWO

(TONY)

Putting my clients on hold for the next couple of days wasn't an easy task to do. Between court dates and meetings, getting away was what I needed. Cindy my secretary handles all arrangements for me, from my clients on down to getting a rental car. Me and the guys all have cars, but we refuse to put unwanted miles on them, so we all decided on the rental car. Now trying to get away from my lady friends will be a challenge that I wasn't ready for. Denise Carter was the girl I always hang out with, I met Denise when I was vacationing in Mexico. Monica Lucas was my stay home and chill girl. Chilling with Monica was a good thing, because the love making was off the chain and her cooking was the best. Sherry, Pam, and Erica were just friends that I could call on for some fun. With Denise and Monica, I would tell in person the other girls I could get away it over the phone. When I pulled up at Denise's house, she was standing in the doorway looking at me with a big smile on her face. Denise was dark skin, stood about 5 foot 8 and thick to deaf. She was good wifey material for somebody else not for me. The word marriage wasn't even in my vocabulary, when mentioned I'd run and never look back. The one girl that I would have married walked away from me when I was in college, her name was Michelle Thomas. Michelle ended up pregnant our last year in college and told me she was having an abortion and leaving school. No matter what I said she still left and me ever loving anybody left with her too. After talking to Denise and getting in a quickie, I was on my way over to Monica's townhouse. Monica didn't know I was coming over so to my surprise Monica had company. Her parents and sister were over having a family meeting and dinner. Really wasn't in the mood to meet anybody parents, but it's too late now. When Monica finish introducing me to everybody, I whispered in her ear we need to talk. Leading me to her bedroom for some privacy, as she walked in front of me that firm ass moving from side to side. When we entered the room, she pulled me in and closed the door behind me. Monica was a gorgeous pecan brown complexion, hazel eyes, with the hourglass body. When she looked at me, she always had a serious, but sexy look that always got to me. As I explain that I'll be gone for a few days, she said OKAY and pulled me on her body, saying let me give you something to think about on your trip. After getting me groove on with Monica, I said my goodbyes to everyone and left. I called Omar and made sure everything was still a go, Shamekia answered the phone. She's Omar oldest daughter, and Diamond is the baby. It was a privilege that Omar and Tosha asked me to be their godfather first, I was so excited, because they asked me instead of the other guys, but eventually Louis and Mike would be asked too, but I was the first one. Omar and Tosha were the perfect couple then. When Shamekia was born Omar was so happy, he had wanted a boy, but a healthy girl would do. Mike was the first one at the hospital, because Omar couldn't remember no one number, he claimed. Because he was so nervous. Before Shamekia was born we all had to be escorted out of the delivery room, doctor only wanted Omar in the room, so we sat patiently in the waiting room. Picture three grown men waiting for a little girl entrance into this world. All my brothers were there that day, Louis wasn't out chasing after a girl and Mike wasn't on the block hustling. I was the one that Omar counted on, who would have thought that Mike would have done what he did. Sometimes circumstances make us step up and do thing that's out of the ordinary.

CHAPTER THREE

(LOUIS)

On my way to see my ex-Felicia, to pick up a couple of clothes I left over her house a few weeks ago. It was a last-minute choice, but I wanted to see if I could give her a quick tune up. Felicia was Mike's first cousin and I had been on and off with her for the past ten years. Felicia knew everything about me, sometimes I think that she knows me better than I know myself. She was the wifey type, but not for me. She's a sexy caramel skin tone with a body to kill for. When I arrived at her house, she came to the door, with nothing on, opening the door and walking away, showing me that coke bottle frame from the back. I politely followed her . After an hour of trying to do everything, we could imagine to each other. The sex was so good that I just laid there, wondering why we broke up, and then reality kick in and here she comes with all kinds of questions about us going to pick up Mike. Even know Mike was her first cousin, she wasn't close to him like that, so if she wanted to know something about Mike, she should ask him. All the time he was locked up she never asked about him. Now he's getting out she wants to ask about him, some cousin she is. So, I just told he straight up, ask Mike. She looked at me crazy, kissed me and said that's why I can't stand you in a playful way. When I was getting ready for round two, the phone rang. Damn forgot that I was supposed to pick Nicole up from the airport, so I told Felicia, I'll give her a rain check and left. Her lying there butt naked without looking back. After picking Nicole up we headed to her house. I still had til morning before with left to pick Mike. After showering with Nicole, I was ready for a few rounds with her. The love making wasn't intense like it was with Felicia. After all these years of going out with all kinds of girls, I could never get Felicia out of my system. Making it home just in time to pack, shower and get in a quick nap. Lying in the bed before going to sleep, I thought all what the weekend we going to be like. Out of the seven years Mike was locked down, I only went and seen him a couple of times, because I didn't want to see him locked up like a caged animal. Me, myself was used to seeing Mike free and wild, not the person prison had made him. When we use to hang out, Mike was the one that taught me the ropes. He was the hustler out the crew, and the one that had all the girls around him all the time. Mike was never seen with the same female when we use to take trips and our little getaways. Mike was on some soul-searching stuff now, so I really don't know what to expect. He's my brother so whatever life he chooses I will still love him. If only Mike knew things had changes for everybody. We all had to become better men for Omar. We all had to step to the plate and really have his back as brothers.

(The Ride) (Omar)

After picking up Tony and Louis the trip was on. I could feel the tension in the SUV, Louis was busy texting and Tony just was staring into space. I broke the silence, letting them know that our brother, that has been gone seven long years is coming home, a day that all have waited on. What happen in the past is just that, the past. Time to move on to bigger and better things. Tony said I can't believe that he's finally coming home, these last couple of days I really haven't the time to let my mind think about Mike coming home, but now the day is finally here. It doesn't really seem like it been seven long years. A lot has changed since Mike left Louis mumbled me and Mike was wild boys back then chasing every woman we seen. Mike never did have a main girl, so I was surprised when he told me that Tiffany, had been visiting and writing him. Omar, as I remember Tiffany was one of Tosha's friends right yes Omar answered they went to college together and Tiffany help me with the girls from time to time. I think that she's good for Mike, she has her own house, nice job, and she knows what she wants out of life. She's her own woman, don't need a man to define her, a good woman these days is hard to find, Louis let slip out, trying to catch himself. No, they're not hard to find, it's just you're not really looking Omar replied. Everybody knew that Louis was a player, but something about him and Felicia we didn't understand. He always run back to her when he was in trouble or just wanted to talk, and she always was there for him no matter what, so when the questions come up about Felicia and him, he never really answered, he just says that they're good. It's been three years since my wife Tosha passed away. Every time me and the guys get together, I feel her presence, because she was the reasoning voice for us. Mike really took her death hard because he was locked up and couldn't do nothing for her. The cancer had spread over fifty percent of her body, and it wasn't anything that the doctors could do. Tosha made it clear that she would be the one to tell Mike, so the day after she got the news from the doctor, she left out alone to tell Mike. Tosha never really shared what her and Mike talked about, but we know that, whatever was said changed Mike completely. That's when him and Tiffany got tight. The guys always ask me could I ever date another woman, and I'd tell them I don't know, but right now my focus is the girls. To me Tosha was my life, everything that I ever planned included her know she's gone, for the first couple of years I was lost. Nothing the guys said could stop the pain and resentment I felt. I blamed everybody I could, but then one day I received a letter from Mike. He answered a lot of question that was in my head, that I shared with no one. It was like Mike had felt all the pain I felt, and that letter gave me strength to get through. Tony touched me on my shoulder, bringing me back to the conversation we were having. Tony just looked at me, nothing had to be said. Tony changed the subject, and asked Louis, did Mike know about him and Felicia, and if he did how he felt about sleeping with his cousin. Louis didn't answer at first, but then tried to explain. Yes and no, he knows that we communicate, but he doesn't know that we're sleeping together. So how are you going to explain that to Mike. I don't know yet Tony but when I come up with the answer you will be the first to know. Omar laughed out saying, somebody got some explaining to do. Louis just answered Mike will understand and who knows Felicia may be the one. When Louis said that I like to run off the road. What the hell Omar blurted out. Omar I've been thinking about this for a while now, maybe Mike's preaching to me is working. Mike coming home to find me doing the same as he left, made me really look at myself and my life. I may have a house, cars and money in the bank, but every night I spend alone. The only person that's been making me feel whole is Felicia. When I'm with her I'm good, I feel that we could take it to the next level, I'm saying I want a family of my own. Omar and Tony look at each other shocked, was they really hearing Louis right. I see that Louis is finally going up. The car was silence for a minute, and we just tried to take everything in what I just heard. Then out of nowhere Louis asked Tony was he still choosing his business over starting a family. Being a good lawyer means staying on top of everything. He was hands on in all his business dealing and treated his clients with respect. Ever since Tony won a big company lawsuit. Tony looked back at Louis and answered, maybe the time is not right for me. I am getting ready to expand my business taking on partners. Starting to take on criminal cases so right now I'm real busy. I always wanted to do criminal justice after Mike got railroad with his case. But believe me Louis after this I will be ready to start me a family too. You guys are talking like you're in your twenties, we're not spring chickens anymore, the time is now. In a couple of years both of you will be knocking on forty, so the both of you really don't have much time, Omar explains. Louis it's good that you're ready but are you really ready. You just slept with Felicia then, went and slept with Nicole. That doesn't sound like a man ready to settle down. Tony I'm so tired of you making excuses with this business. We have made enough money investing in stocks. We all can stop working today and live like we want to live. Me myself just think that you guys are scared to commit to that one woman. Scared that you might like it and become family men. I have sat back and watched you two with my daughters, you guys are good with them, you're all they talk about the uncles. You two will make good dads but first you must find that right woman. To make you want to change. When I met Tosha, I knew she was the one. She lite up my life, everything about her I loved. When I do decide to date again, my search for a woman wouldn't never be modeled like Tosha. She would have to have her own sense of purpose in life. It's not just about me, Shamekia and Diamond would play a part in this too because, my choices reflect on their lives too. When people date and find out that they're not meant for each other, look at where you leave the kids at. My kids are my world right now, they're the air that I get up every morning to breathe. Their smiles are what keep me going every day. Being mancho left me when my wife died. I had to become dad and mom, not by choice, but by force. Forced to take on responsibilities that men are not use too, never planned on rising my girls alone, I took for granted thinking that she would always be here. But God sure changed that. Sorry I went there guys, but I've watch you guys run through women like toys. I constantly remind you both that your godfather's to my two daughters and you still don't get it. Mike coming home and you guys are still running around here like men with no purpose. Tell me what kind of advice you got tell give Mike, other than, what's the hottest club scene or where the finest girls hang out. Mike did something while he was gone, he really found his self something the both of you have to do. Louis don't get me wrong; you sound like you're on the right track but how sincere are you. Can you really give up Nicole and other women in your life to settle down and marry Felicia, or you just feeling guilty because Mike is coming home and you haven't told him about you and Felicia, and you Tony, you can't stay away from your job long enough to meet a good woman. The ones you do find time to go out with, ninety percent of the time you are standing them up or making excuses. You two guys are a piece of work, single black men with something to offer and here you are wasting time by being blind to your own life crisis. If I'm wrong tell me and I'll apologize to you, but that won't happen because you know I'm right. I'm not a person on the street talking behind your back I'm being a friend and telling you to your face. Louis give me some of your input on what I'm saying. Well, I have had bad choice in women over the years and I can't take the blame all by myself. Didn't always be like this, certain situations can change anybody. True, Felicia is a good woman, but she hurt me in the beginning. She was my heart and soul, trusted her with every piece of my heart, she took that from me by lying and cheating on me. Back then she wanted something I couldn't give her. She wanted marriage something that was far from my mind. Felicia was the first woman that I ever loved. When I caught her with another guy something inside me went numb. Numb to trust, to give anybody that much control and power over me ever again. It's true I dated women before her, but my emotions weren't into any of them. Felicia just recently told me, that the reason she cheated was because of past experiences I had with other women. The way I treated them, she heard about it and thought that I would do her the same. We both shared somethings that we both should've been open with conversation towards each other instead of guessing and asking other people. That's why I acted towards women like I did, because me being a man didn't really know who to take it. Felicia is a part of the good and bad that's inside of me. Nicole just somebody that won't let me go. I've tried to leave her alone, but she's threatened to hurt me and her, she's even called Felicia a couple of times. After we get through with Mike, I'm going to sit Felicia down and put everything on the line again. No more games, everything you said is true Omar. Tony, you're quiet, what kind of excuses you have speak up. I can't lie, I love making money, and I enjoy company with different females. When it's time for me to settle down, I will but right now, let me do me. This trip is not about relationships, it's about picking up Mike from prison and hanging out like old times. Omar snapped, Tony this is not old times we're all grown now, those days are over with, people change, lives change I've change. I myself can't run around and do what I use to. My life made me grow up and become a man when I already thought I was. You've seen firsthand at what me and Mike went through when Mike did what he did for me, I owe him my life two times over. Tony, your day is coming and when it does, I will be there to see how you handle it. Remember everything not always going to be peaches and cream. You will meet that one woman, and she will change every simple thought you ever had. Okay I'm done with my preaching for now, two hours before I'm there, both of yall get some rest, I'll wake yall when we get to the prison.

The Reunion

After driving for a couple of hours while the guys slept, we finally made it. The sun was just peeking out behind the morning clouds. When we pulled up to the prison, the guard at the booth told me to pull around and park and that Mike will be out in a few minutes. Before I could put the car into park, there was Mike walking towards us with a big smile on his face. The expression on his face said everything. By now Louis and Tony was up and getting out of the truck. All the wait was over, my brother was free. We all were in the middle of the parking lot embracing Mike one by one. Smiles turning into tears, men letting their real emotions show and not afraid who sees. When the silence broke, Mike said joking, it took us long enough and we all got in the truck. As I was pulling away leaving the prison, Mike was looking at a window, saying in a quiet voice goodbye old friend take care. No one said a word we all waited for Mike, but he remained silent until we got on the highway. It was Thursday and Mike wouldn't have to report to his parole officer until Monday, so we had planned a little weekend getaway for Mike.

Mike didn't ask any question about where we were headed, he just laid his head back and closed his eyes. After about ten minutes Mike said in relax voice, it's good to be out of that place. So glad to be chilling in person with my brothers. Louis Louis Louis, so what's up with you and my cousin Felicia, Louis looked at Mike in amazement but before he answered, Mike spoke, I've known for a long time that you and Felicia was messing around. She called me and asked for my permission to go out with you. She didn't want to come between us, and it was all about a respect thing to her. At first, I didn't agree but you're both adults so why would I stand in the way. I waited for you to come to me, but you never did. I give you the benefit of doubt and said that you must have your reason, so I didn't worry, but just know for the record I knew. Louis tried to explain but Mike waved him off. Omar stepped in to loosen. The tension by, asking Mike what his plans are. I'm just going to go with the flow. My parole address is at Tiffany's, so I won't be staying with any of you. Before you say anything Omar, I'm sure about this, she's my Tosha it's somethings that I have to do, remember I've been gone for the last seven years, everybody else life was still going on and mines was put on hold. Out of all the women I use to mess with Tiffany was the only one that stayed down. Loyalty means everything to me; you guys know that. Omar, I like to thank you and the girls coming seeing me faithful even though yall was going through hell, but I can't understand where my other two brothers was. They must have families I know nothing about to keep them away, what do you have to say Tony. I've been busy trying to get my business up and running. So, it takes seven years to get your business up and running and what about the weekends. I sent money Mike, I thought that would be enough, I tried to make myself come, but just didn't want to see you locked up like some animal. What about you Louis what is your excuse. No excuse just the truth, my picture of you, is you being free, not locked up in a cell. When I came and seen you those few times, when I left, found myself at the nearest liquor store drinking and talking to myself, I hated that feeling Mike, I'm truly sorry bro. Louis, I feel you because the first time you came, you couldn't stop crying, but Tony you have no excuse. I know about all your weekend vacation with all those different women, the truth is you was in your own world, Omar kept my filled in on everything. Tony, you really disappointed me, but you're still my brother and still have much love for you. Louis now, what are your plans with my little cousin. When I left the streets, you were a player, so what's the deal. Mike ever since I've been dating Felicia, she's been my heart, we've had our ups and downs. We still have a lot of things to sit down and work out but, I do think we can make it. That player you're talking about met somebody that played his heart, I'm all played out bro. What you think Omar, Mike asked. I've been talking to Louis, and he seems to be for real about Felicia. Louis says he's wants his own family. Okay so Tony the only one still out there playing, thinking life goes on forever, taking each moment for granted. It's not like that Mike, just haven't met no one that I wanted to settle down with. So why do you keep parading these women around family around Diamond and Shamekia especially. They don't need to see that. Where's your parenthood at, what kind of example you're sitting for them Tony. Omar should have been said something to you about that. You're really wrong for that Tony. Omar, I went to go to a nice restaurant with you and my nieces and then I'm going to Tiffany's, that weekend getaway you have plan cancel it. Been on a getaway long enough, I just need plenty of family and friends around me. Sorry fellas, that life is over for me, life is too short to keep putting off what you can do today tomorrow. These seven years away has taught me to stop taking everything for granted. The talked I had with Tosha open my eyes to a lot of bullshit we were doing, prison played a part too. Seeing young men in there with life sentences, haven't even started to live life yet. Looking in their eyes and seeing emptiness that they endure every day because of the choices they made. Some of them virgins, never been with a woman, not only that never learning to drive or live in your own house, but that's also what made me change my life. A person can only take so much and realize that something I'm doing not right. Mr. Rod seen the pain I was feeling looking at these young men. Mr. Rod was a preacher that murder a man for raping his daughter, his serving twenty-years for manslaughter and his been locked up fifteen years. He sat me down and explained things to me that I needed to hear. Before I get into all that let's stop and get something to eat. Where do you want to go asked Omar, to a steakhouse Mike response? Omar tried to talk Mike into going on with the plans they had for the weekend, but he still refused and let them know that it would be plenty of time for that, right now he just wanted to chill with us for a little while and then go home to Tiffany. Louis asked how serious are you and Tiffany? I mean you never talked about her when you was dating her. She was there when I needed someone to tell me the truth about things, regardless of where I was, and wasn't afraid if it hurt my feelings or not. When she came to visit me, she seen me as I was, a man that was trying to find his purpose in life. She grabbed my attention and didn't let go. Tiffany made me fall in love with her without even trying. Tiffany touched a place in me I didn't knew existed. Before her, things weren't easy for me, but now, things are much clearer and acceptable. Tiffany took my mind off my circumstances and made me check myself. Every time we were together, I felt complete and a different person. Let me share something that may help you try to understand why I'll looking at life like this now. When I left the county jail, my first stop was Jackson Diagnostics. This is the same prison that house death row inmates. Crazy how my cell was located, sat right across from death row. Every day the same scenery for two months. Seeing some of those guys on death row, body language made me think about everything I ever done in the past. I wonder how those guys felt, knowing that they're never going to be free again, that their only freedom on consisted of death. In a situation like that, it takes a strong-minded person to endure that. We as men sometimes put ourselves in predicaments that takes us out of our safe element. I could have been one of those guys easily. Somebody prayed hard enough for me to save my life. My mom and dad died while in prison, so just think what I went through, no disrespect to you guys, but when the lights are turned off and silence kicks in, that's when the pain starts. Standing up there at the grave site knowing in the next few hours you'll be back behind bars again with only my thoughts. Thoughts became my worst enemy until I learn to control them. See it gets deeper than this, I haven't even scratched the surface, yet. Omar stops at the first steakhouse you see all this talking has really made me hungry. Before we get off the subject Mike, why didn't you let me and the guys know what you were going through Omar asked, because it was my battle to fight, when all said and done I was still in prison doing time. You guys could only due so much, a lot of things I had to learn and do on my own. To become the man that I needed to be, meant that the man I became had to die.

Mike and Omar

Louis and Tony sit at the bar at Longhorns to order a few drinks, while Mike and Omar find a table and order the food. Mike, I never did thank you for taking that manslaughter charge for me. Omar, bro we agreed to never discuss. It's over, let it die. I can't, you give up seven years of your life for me. All because my wanting to prove a point. Do you ever regret taking that charge for me? Why do we have to talk about this now? Because it's been on my mind real heavy for the last couple of years and every time, I bring it up, you blow my off. Okay Omar let's talk, I've buried that night in my mind a long time ago, I didn't only do it for you, your family and future is what I did it for. If it would have been one of the other guys, we wouldn't be having this conversation. Me and Tosha talked about this when she came and seen me in prison. We talked about her being sick but, mainly we talked about you. She made me promise to take care of you. And to help ??? the girls. She knew that our bond was deeper. Tosha tried best she could ??? explain how you changed her life. You were her first love. When you came in her life it sparked something inside of her. Everything seems to just fall into place. Everything that the two of you did together??? Do you still wake up in the middle of the night apologizing to her, yea bro. She told me about those dreams. If I had to do it all over again, I'll do it, simply because I love the person I've become. Maybe this was meant to happen, only God knows, but what has been done been done. Tosha mention when she visited you that something was going on with you, but she didn't say what. Omar, you got to forget about all those thoughts about that night. Because the girls need all your attention, not something that happen in the past, that everybody is trying to forget. I've missed out in a lot of time already so let's enjoy life. Omar bowed his head, okay for now

Mike. Louis and Tony left the bar when the food arrived. Everybody ate in silence until Mike asked to use Omar phone. Mike made the call-in front of all the guys he calls Tiffany to let her know that he was out and okay. Mike explained to Tiffany that he had a change of plans, and that he wouldn't be in until Sunday. Before he could get another word out, Tiffany told him to stop, that she'll be there waiting on him and that she knew you're going to have to change, and that mean letting go of all the nonsense. Omar I just need some time to think. Time to think you've had forty years to think get out my car Tony and grow up.

Omar
Thoughts

In times of silence, I catch myself thinking about how, I could of did things better. As men was sometimes think that we're super-men, always thinking that we can't be hurt and when it happens, we want to put the blame on everything and everybody knowing deep inside who's really the blame. My friends seen me at my weakest. They had to watch their close friend lose the one thing that he loved most in the world taken away, and again they stood and watched me slowly rebuild my life. As a man I've found out that we don't have control over everything. When disaster hits, just like everybody else. We get nervous ourselves. We try to put on an act to be strong but, when we're alone, emotions can't be held back. Everybody hurts and they handle it different. Some turn to God, some turns to things that makes them numb, I turn to friends. Without my friends I would have lost my mind. But I learned something else too, that God plays a role in our lives. When I realize who God was, my wife was God. Louis and Tony don't know that Mike's not the same. They're too busy to really sit down and talk to Mike, they're end for a big surprise. Mike explained to me what changes had occurred in his life on one Sunday, I visited him alone. He sat in front of me and poured his heart out about his past. Things he shared I never imagine someone could go through so much. He shared things that him and Tosha talked about when she told him about her illness. My wife illness changed his life. Real men I been hearing that all my life. Everybody has a different opinion about what real men means but to me it's a man who's not scared to get on his knees and ask for God's help.

After dropping Mike and Louis off, that left the door open. For me and Tony to have a one-on-one conversation. Wanted to know what was really going on it that head of his. Before taking him home, we just rode around the city. Tony broke the ice first staying Mike was really change for the best. Yea, you can say that. Omar, do you remember when I use to date Michelle Thomas? Yes, where is she at now, didn't you and her go to the same college. She's a lawyer now right. Well, she was but Ms. Thomas is a judge now. What ever happen between you two. We dated for three years we both was busy with our careers, so we tried to spend time together whenever we had a chance. Things had picked up for both of us and it was hard trying to find time to spend together. We became distant, the phone calls had cease between the two of us, and eventually we drifted apart. A few months goes by, and Michelle calls me out the blue, crying saying she need to talk to me as soon as possible. So, I met her at an apartment she shared with her girlfriend. When I walked through the door Michelle had a look on her face sort of surprise me. We sat down and begin to have small talk, hey how you doing? how the family etc., etc. then she grabbed me by the hand and said, I'm four months pregnant and you're the father. At first, I didn't know what to say, just sat there shocked, mad and happy at the same time. First thing she said was she wasn't having it and that she was going to get an abortion in the morning. The abortion never happened, at least I thought it did until a year ago when I ran across her at Lenox mall shopping with my daughter. Come to find out she didn't have that abortion. So, when I approached her about it, she gave me her number and told me to meet her later because this wasn't the place to talk about what she had to say. So, I'm pissed on how she trying to play me, and I just told her straight up right there, that she wasn't getting out of my eyesight and that I need answers now. So, we went and talked in her car. Michelle told me that she decided to have Keisha "my daughter" on her own because she felt like I wasn't ready to be a dad. So, we went back and forth until she told me that she didn't want me to be a part of her life until I knew what I wanted in life. Damn bro, you are telling me you have a daughter that you didn't know about. Yes, Omar she's five years old and look just like me. Michelle is playing hard ball, she won't get me get her by myself until my lifestyle changes that's why I've been working so hard, trying to show her that my shits together. Do she know that you're one of the girl's godfather's, yes, but she doesn't believe all that, she really thinks I'm still that same guy. Well Mike what have you showed her beside you're getting your business together. Have you showed her that you have your own place, what have you done to change her mind? Be honest Tony are you really ready to enter this little girl's life and be there like you're suppose to. Can you give up chasing the women and stop partying? In order for Michelle to let you spend time alone with your daughter. Me and the fellas have had some long nights on these courts. Basketball was our escape from the madness around us. Each one of us all went through some things growing up, being there for each other is how we made it through. Now here we are all grown up still here for each other. Regardless how bad I disagree with their ways; I could never turn my back on them. Looking at the guys shooting basketball at our old court, made me realize that a new era of our lives has just begun.

Mike and Tiffany

Mike knock on Tiffany house door, before he could try to knock again, she opens the door with tears in her eyes. What a surprise Mike, what are you doing here. I'm coming home if that's okay with you. Babe, Tiffany stepped to the side and whispered what are you waiting for come in. Before he got in the doorway good, she grabbed him and pulled Mike close to her, put her hands on his face and kissed him. Mike's hands eased around her waist and held her like she was the last woman on earth. Standing and kissing in the middle of the door, Tiffany paused long enough to shut the door. Leading Mike to the couch, she asked, I thought you had plans. Mike explains to Tiffany what changed his mind, and before he knew it, she was on top kissing him again. Tiffany whispered in Mike's ear, I know you said you wanted to wait before we made love to each other, but I change my mind, please let me have you right now. Mike hesitated and gave in to request. Mike got on top of Tiffany and slowly removing her clothes never taking his eyes from hers. Tiffany tried to get Mike to go faster, but he still moves show. Every time he put his lips to her, Tiffany would lose control of her body movements shaking and trembling like she never done before. Tiffany gasping for air, what are you doing to me. Going to take my fingers and caress you all over until you're at my mercy. Every place Mike kissed he gently blew his warm breath causing to shiver uncontrollably, over and over he played with Tiffany until she couldn't take anymore and played Mike until he was on his back now. Now my turn she said in a seductive voice. I've been waiting to touch you all over baby, let me give you what you've been missing. Close your eyes and relax Mike baby. She begins sucking on Mike's neck, rubbing her hands on any part and removing clothes at the same time. Mike begins to breathe in deep. Taking everything, she was dishing out to him. Whispering in Mike ear, do you want me as bad as I want you, bladder make answered, promise to love me Mike, yes Tiffany, give me what I need Mike, what's that baby, you inside me not yet, why, something I want from you, what's that Mike, give me a baby, anything you want, just make love to me. Mike slid his manhood into Tiffany wetness, every thrust she gasp for air, scratching her nails deep into Mike skin, Tiffany became wetter and wetter as things intense between the two of them, each one trying to get the better of the other Tiffany cumming back to back studiedly grinding on make harder and harder making his hard dick stand up deep inside of hot and wet pussy, and Mike whispered cumming baby, Tiffany open up to take in all his seed in her, still grinding hard as she could. Tiffany falls on my chest, ???? herself in his arms. This is where I want to be, promise me you'll never leave again Mike. All we talked about over the years, your, her so let's make it happen for us. I'll give you all the babies you want, just give me you all, be true to me. Tiffany, I promise to you before this week is out, you'll be my wife, just like we planned. This feels good "love". Remember when I just up and called you when I was in county, and you accepted my called. We talked about what I did to cause you to walk away from me. You said that I wasn't capable of loving nobody. We've talked every day since and we've shared our deepest thoughts and secrets with each other. Beside Omar, I can truly say you've become my closest friend. Mike same here, for a long time I really thought that you were just talking jail talk, but the more we talked the more I seen ordinary man become an extraordinary man. A man I seen a future with. And now you're here in my arms, in our house, I'm good baby. Tears begin to roll down Tiffany face. Mike was the man she been longing for, but because of Mike being Mike back then she had to walk away or lose herself. That night Mike called her from jail, she seized the moment by just being a listening ear. By doing so Mike opens up to her in ways she only dreamed a man would. Tosha knew that I was crazy about him, and eventually I found out that it was her who told Mike to call. He was just two years into a seven-year sentence. Mike asked me if I ever deal with a man that was locked up, no he was the first. We started off just talking on the phone and I asked him to put me on his visitation list. They had just shipped him to a state prison in Macon. It was an hour and a half drive from Atlanta. Visitation was every Saturday, Sunday and all the holidays. Started off just Saturdays, then things begin to get serious between us, and I couldn't see him enough. Saturday and Sundays I was there every week for four years, including all holidays. Somewhere between the phone calls, letters and visitation I fell madly in love with Mike. Never cried over the phone to a man that I had to wait four years to be with. Why are you thinking about Tiffany, just letting my mind wonder about things to come? Baby a lot of good things are instore for us. Tiffany I've been gone for a while so I'm behind a little baby I need you to catch up on things. I'm leaving out in the morning, and I'll be back Monday morning. We can do everything that we need to do after I check in with the parole officer. Mike, I have something to show you in the bedroom. We both got up from the couch and headed up stairs. First time seeing Tiffany house wasn't a shock to me because in my mind I had already been here, when I walked into the room Tiffany pointed to the closet, to my surprise she had gotten all my clothes from my mom's house, shoes ties, socks jewelry, I mean everything I own was at her house. Tiffany had a chance to meet my mom before she passed, every Sunday after she left from visiting me, she would go by and sit with my mom. After my mom passed away, she locked the house up made sure all the bills and things were paid. Before I could turn around to say thanks to Tiffany, she pulled out two letters address to me, one was from my mom and the other from Tosha. They were still sealed and not open. Both of them made me promise not to give them to you until you came home. I pushed the letters to the side and pulled Tiffany on the bed where I was. After hours of love making, we both fell asleep. Waking up in the middle of the night, looking at the letters wondering what was so important that I couldn't open them until I got home.

The Weekend Getaway

After being up all night with Shamekia and Diamond getting up to them fixing me breakfast really got my day started. They had a thousand questions about their Uncle Mike, so I agreed to let them ride went me to pick him up. When Mike came to the car halfway sleep the girls jumped out of the truck almost knocking Mike down, with hugs and kisses. Seeing Mike and the girls in tears words can't explain. Can't remember the last time the girls laughed liked this. They talked as I drove back to drop the girls off to the aunt. All three of them made all kinds of plans and things to do when we returned from our little trip. I myself couldn't wait to get Mike to his self to see how the night went. After the girls said their goodbyes, we and Mike drove off leaving them in the driveway waving. Looking at Mike smiling, how did last night go, with a sharp grin on his face, everything went good Omar, Tiffany woke me up with all kinds of presents like it was my birthday. New clothes, a cell phone that I don't have a clue about and a watch that's probably going to get me robbed. Well, she seems to be on top of things. Gave you that phone so she can keep tabs on you she's just like Tosha, thinks everything through, Tiffany makes sure all her eyes are dotted and tees are crossed. Omar man, she cried when I left this morning. Omar how did our investments work out. Well glad you asked, meant to tell you yesterday, with all the interest, just look in the dashboard at your bank statement. Wow Omar we did very good. The money from your mom and dad insurance policies are in another account. So, you're saying I have more money yes, my brother you do, welcome to the mile high club. After we get back, we need to go ring shopping for Tiffany. Promised her when I got back that we're getting married. Why so fast Mike. This is something that me and her put on hold for a year now. She wanted to marry me while in jail, but that wasn't what she really wanted. I'll fill you in on the details later, because you and my nieces are going to help me pull this romantic simple wedding off. Just you me the girls Tiffany and the pastor. You know I'm down for whatever as long as you know what you're doing. So what's new Omar, man Tony dropped a bomb on me last night. He'll tell you when I scoop him and Louis up. What did Tony do or say now. Nothing man he's going to blow you out of the water with what's going on with him. Mike is Tiffany real cool with you leaving for the weekend. So, you're not going to tell me what you and Tony talked about, no I'm going to let him tell you. Okay, Tiffany cool, we talked this morning before you called to pick me up. If she was upset about it, she was hiding it good. Omar, Tiffany did her thang to me last night, really this trip almost got canceled, and then what she did to me before you pulled up, man man, man. When we dated before it wasn't intense like it is now. The first time we had sex before I got locked up was just that sex, but feelings are involved now and when I say we made love to each other, okay okay Mike a little too much information. Omar this woman is going to be my wife before this week is out. Bro as long as you're good I'm good, I'm truly happy for you, but while we're alone, I've been holding something on my chest for a long time I want to share with you. When me and Tosha, first met she told me that she was just getting out of an abusive relationship and that she fears for her life. She had him locked up and was going back and forth to court. Well, he ended up getting ten years. He tried to get in contact with her through his friends, but he got no response. So, when he found out that she was with me, his boys started sending me threats. By thing I had fallen in love with Tosha, and she was pregnant with Shamekia. There was no way that I could just leave. So, we got the police involved and things seem to die down, until her ex-Todd Smith came up for parole, but before he could make parole, they called Tosha and interviewed her over the phone. After the conversation they had with Tosha, they denied his parole and he had to do the remainder of his sentence. So, in other words he had five more years to do. The threats started coming in again this time worst. Remember when I just up and moved further out from the city, well that was the reason. Mike what if, stop right there Omar. Once again, what's done is done. We can't change what happen or get back the time I spent in prison. I've moved on from it and you should too. So really let that go Omar, please bro. Nothing you say can make me undo what I did. Me and Tosha had the somewhat same conversation, I did what needed to be did and it was one of the best decisions I ever made. It changed my life for the better, I'm not that wild young man running around thinking like most black men that the world owes them something. The world doesn't owe us anything. Being at the stage of my life doesn't make me smarter or better than the next man, it just makes me more of a complete man with his eyes wide open. When we start seeing past the shining lights and glamor and try to understand how to enjoy a simple sunrise. Mike where is all this coming from, what happen to you in that place, life Omar life. You asked where all this coming is from, it comes from a place when a man's self-respect has been ran through the mud and stepped on. Omar I've seen grown man break down and cry their eyes out, to losing family members, to wives walking out of their lives to being wrongly accused, if you think you have a bad story, believe me there's somebody out there with one worst. Like I said we take a simple sunrise for granted. Thinking it's always going to be there for us to see, some guys some places will never see their son again. Mothers are walking into empty rooms never to be occupied by her son again. Shamekia Diamond and the baby that me and Tiffany trying to make, will understand how to enjoy the simple. Don't mean to cut you off, but you're trying already to make a family with Tiffany. Started last night. I'm speechless bro. Mike why is the police Louis and Tony standing outside talking in front of Louis house. Omar walks over to Louis to see what's going on. Mike sees Felicia talking to a lady officer and immediately jumps out the car. As his walking towards Felicia, Louis looks up and follow behind him. By the time Mike gets to Felicia the lady officer is walking off. What's up cuz, are you okay, before she could answer Louis cuts in. Everything under control, somebody flat all the tires on both my cars. Excuse us Louis, but I need to speak to Felicia alone. Cuz why are you shaking like that. Mike I'm okay, just tired of this craziness with one of Louis ex-girlfriend. Okay since me and Louis decided to be together, she's been stalking and threating to hurt us. We filed restraining papers against her, but it seems like that just made things worst. Not only do she know where I stay, she also knows where I work also. What is Louis doing about this, is he really finished with this girl. He says it's over and I truly believe him. We've been talking about moving together but we got to handle this first. Sorry Mike I didn't come see you as much as I should have, don't worry about that at least you come. You're my family Felicia always remember that I love you cuz, I'll talk to you when I return from this trip. After Louis finish talking to the police, he explains to everybody what happen. Felicia left to go home but decided to go stay at a friend's house until Louis returned from his trip. Looking over at Mike to see what was going on in his mind. Felicia's his cousin and somehow, he has right to be upset. Louis tried to explain to Mike that he really was serious about Felicia and that he'll never put her in harm's way, that Nicole was someone he dated before he decided to make things work out between him and Felicia. Mike remains silent looking and Mike turn to the window. Suddenly Mike turn to Louis saying, just handle your business Louis, before someone really gets hurt. There's no telling what that girl Nicole is capable of. With everything going on Omar was the only one seeing Tony talking to himself. What's up Tony. Just got something on my mind Omar. We boys Tony you can talk to us about anything, so he begins to explain what was going on between him and Michelle. When he got home last night, she was sitting in his driveway waiting for him. She explains why she'd been treating him so bad about the whole situation. She had been letting her fears of her childhood dictate her future. Michelle watched her daddy send her mother through. Pure hell, mental abuse and physical abuse she seems first hand and had to endure all that come with that. The feelings that she felt when she got older about man. How she really couldn't really trust any man. Michelle let Tony know that she had been going to counseling. She was there to apologize for how he been getting treated. Tony ride to her and spent the night with and Keisha his daughter. So, Tony you got to be with your daughter why the worried look on your face? Because I had sex with her last night and when I tried to leave Michelle got all upset. Tony, you know having sex only complicate matters. True that Omar but trying to explain to a woman that's been through hell when she was a child can be a little tough. She has her mind set on having a family, but it must be her way and her way only right now. A simple man could go for that but I'm not simple. If she just meets me halfway on some things, I could go for that but. Tony you've been holding back on us, Mike said with a grin on his face. Do you have any feelings whatsoever for this woman? Yes, I did at one time, until she just up and disappeared on me. But what about now Tony? Mixed feelings Omar, she broke my heart one time, can't give her that chance again. We'll let her know Omar yelled out. I'm going to sit down and put everything on the table after this trip. Fellas we all got a lot going on let's cancel this trip until we all handled our business, Omar asked. Everybody agrees, so everybody headed back home.

The Week

Louis called Felicia from his cell phone from the car to let her know that the trip had been canceled, and that, he was on his way home and that he'll see her later. After he got off the phone, he dialed Nicole number, to ask her to meet him to talk. Louis realizes in order for him to have any kind of relationship with Felicia, Nicole would really have to be out the picture. He knew that this back and forth between the two-woman had to stop. Before Louis hung the phone up Mike asked him what was he up to. Louis simply told Mike the only way I can get this girl to leave me alone is to really tell her the truth about my feelings for her what Felicia think about this love, she doesn't know Mike. It's something I have to do for myself to. Today this incident showed me what kind of real feelings I had for Felicia. All that kept running through my mind was, what if she hurt Felicia. If she's bold enough to slash tires, what else is she capable of. Do you want me to run with your bro, no that's okay, Nicole not crazy as she thinks? Mike sat back in the seat and didn't say anything else, until Omar asked him to call Tiffany on his new cell phone to let her know you're on your way, not yet Omar, I need you and the girls to go do some shopping with me. We have to start planning something special for Tiffany. So, what do you have in mind Mike? First, I need Shamekia and Diamond help me go pick out the rings, and then we have to find a next quiet area, maybe a public garden with all kinds of flowers. Okay calling the girls now to let them know what's going on. This is going to be a day that Felicia remembers forever. Tony what are your plans for the rest of the day. Going to find Michelle Omar, and really try to get her to understand what she did to me, I never told her, how bad I felt and what it did to my ego. She told me like it was a big thing, I'm pregnant but I'm having an abortion, no feelings on her part at all. And then to find out that the abortion didn't happen, talk about hurt and confused. Tony take it from me, you're not the first man to feel like this, we all go through something or another, some more painful than other, we can't sit back and try to figure how we got into this and who's to blame, but try to accept it, handle it and move on. You're so right Omar, Mike agreed, Tony going to really have to open his heart and let Michelle see the side that she felled in love with years ago, not the person that made her run the first time. I feel what both of you're saying, remembering those days are very simple for me, back then I enjoyed sitting at home on a Friday and Saturday night, chilling watching T.V. on the couch with her. Back then she filled that empty place that's in me now. Today Tony, Michelle really messed with your emotions. Don't make fun of me Louis, this a little too real to me. Sorry about that, it just, you and all this hidden from us. All these different women we see you with, who would of known the reason for it. So, Tony what if she wants to work at starting another relationship, how do you feel about that. To be honest Mike, I really don't know if I could treat her again like that, the pain has resurfaced. Her putting me through this ordeal with my daughter. First, we just need to talk, put everything on the line and go from there. Sounds like a plan Tony, we're all behind you, just let us know. After dropping off Louis and Tony, Omar and Mike went by Tosha's sister to pick the girl up. Shamekia and Robin (Tosha's sister) went online to look at rings and printed some out for Mike to look at. He couldn't decide until he seen the rings in person. Before they went to get the rings, Omar stopped by the bank to have all of Mike's accounts updated and handed them over to Mike. Mike couldn't believe the amount of money that he was seeing in his account. He had enough money to do anything he ever dreamed of. Mike teared up and looked at Omar, Tosha said that you and me, man I love you bro thanks. Never thought in my wildest dreams that I would be in a position like this. When I finally called Tiffany, she was over her friend's house making cocktails. After telling my plans to her she agreed to meet me later at my discretion. Reading all of those romantic novels in prison, may pay off after all. When we left the bank, the jeweler was the next stop. While we were in the bank, the owner gives us a card to one of his brother's stores out in Buckhead. Shamekia couldn't wait, when we pulled up at the store, she jumped out her and Diamond pulling Mike alone. The rings that they see on the internet didn't have nothing on these rings. They finally picked out a ring that you could spot from across the street. The price of the ring didn't matter because Mike had the funds to pay for it. Finishing up paying for the ring. He turned to Shamekia now the fun begins. Mike asked Omar to cook dinner at his house tonight so that, he could propose to Tiffany around him and the girls. Mike knew that Omar was a good cook and would be more than willing to help me pull this off. After running around and making all the arrangements. Doing a little of shopping with the girls, trying to catch up on the latest styles, we finally made it to Omar's house. I really didn't know Tiffany's parents well, but Tiffany had told them about me. Mentioning it to Omar that I would want the parents there without her knowing would be hard. Omar smile, saying, remember Mike, Tiffany's Tosha close friend. I met Tiffany's parents. Me and her dad are golf buddies and the girls occasionally spends the weekend with them. OMG Uncle Mikes talking about Auntie Tiffany, dad, Shamekia asked. Yes Shamekia, and she reaches over and just started hugging Mike crying I'm so glad your home, everything is going to be alright now. What do you mean by that Shamekia and what's wrong? It's just that when mom passes away for a long time, we really didn't have anything happy to be about, until your release day came. Mom told me before she passed what you did for my dad that night. When you got locked up, she told me part of dad got locked up with you until you told him you'll be okay and to stop worrying so much, to concentrate on his family. Uncle Mike's dad never knew that mom told me. Shamekia you kept this in all this time, yes dad, mom said that it would come out on its own at the right time. My baby is growing up into an intelligent beautiful young lady. Do Diamond knows, no never told Diamond, she was just a baby. I love you Uncle Mike you've been my hero for a long time, not just for what you did for dad, but for giving mom the strength she needed to make it when she was about to give up. Yes, dad and Uncle Mike, she told me about you and her talk. Mike and Omar just shook their heads and just sat there in silence. Dads are you forgetting something. Make the call to let Tiffany's parents know and don't forget about Uncle Louis and Tony. Louis was just meeting Nicole when Omar text came in on his cell phone inviting him over for dinner not telling him what for. He waited before he texts back, because Nicole had jumped in the car. What's up Louis, that was real fucked up what you did earlier to my tires. I came to tell you Nicole that I'm done playing the back-and-forth games with you. It should have never gotten to this point. Not only are you causing problems in my life, but others as well. We can't be together. I was honest with you from the beginning, and we agreed that it was just sex, so why all the drama now. Louis I really feel like you played me, Nicole, you put yourself out there like that, you gave me what I wanted, and you knew how I felt about you so how the hell did I play you. Sounds like me you played yourself. Louis I hate man like you, everything you do you think that you're right. Yes, I did think that it could be just sex, but you are paying me to fly this place and that place to be with you, somewhere my feelings get involved, so you're right maybe I did play myself. Sorry it has to be like this Nicole, maybe if I wasn't at this point in my life, it could go on but it's time for me to stop all this. Nicole you're a young beautiful woman, don't waste your time causing me problems. Live your life and find your happiness. I can't believe you Louis, but always remember what goes around comes around. Nicole gets out of the car slamming the door shut without saying a word. Just sat in my car, feeling wrong for how I took advantage of her self-esteem. Felicia really must be working on me, to get something sexy as Nicole to walk away damn. Okay let me text Omar back to let him know I'll be there with Felicia. Omar had called Tony to see how things went with Michelle. He said that he hasn't seen her yet and Omar told him about dinner and asked him to bring her. I'll ask her Omar, but I can't make no promises. Omar started preparing dinner and the girls sat in the kitchen catching Mike up on things. Mike had called Tiffany and told her about dinner. She told her that she was going home to take a little nap change clothes and she'll be there. Little did she know that she was coming to her own engagement dinner. Tiffany had some plans of her own for that night. Tiffany and her girlfriends had went shopping for lingerie. To surprise her man. Tiffany thought to herself, how could I love this man so much. Now that's he's home I'll do my best to keep him happy. Just the simple things that he enjoys with me love him even more. Talking to him about the changes in his life and where he's headed makes me think and say where has this person been all my life. Tiffany glanced over at her watch realizing she had lost track of time rushing out the house. Omar had finishing cooking, and everything was ready. The first two people that arrived at Omar's house was Tiffany's parents. Mike had enough time to sit and talk to them for the first time. Tiffany's parent Shirley and James Jackson was happy to meet Mike. They had heard so much about him from Omar and Tiffany. To them he was the ideal man for their daughter and couldn't be happy, before everybody arrived, all of them sit down and went over the plans on how the night would go. Both Louis and Tony showed up with their dates, even Michelle agreed to come with Tony. Tiffany called to let Mike know that she was pulling in the driveway. Tiffany's parents went upstairs to the den with Shamekia to wait for Mike to send for them. Mike met Tiffany at the door with a big smile on his face. Come in pretty lady, what's up with you. Sorry I'm late baby, lost track of time, your okay baby as long as you made it. Are you hungry, yes what are we having? Steak and lobster are the main course I couldn't tell you what else Omar cooked. Follow me into the living room Tiffany, I have something serious to talk about. Is everything okay Mike, yes just need to talk. By then everybody had gathered into the living room, Tiffany spotted her mom and dad coming down the stairs. She turns to look at Mike who was down on one knee. What are you doing Mike, listen Tiffany? You have held me down for the last seven years. When I thought my world was over you appeared and made my life different. Remember the first visit we had, and you asked me was I through running the streets and my response, was if I found the right woman I would. This night wouldn't be perfect without your parents here to witness and share this night with us. Tears begin to roll down Tiffany face as she fell to her knees with Mike. Tiffany you're that person I want to be with for the rest of my life. If time stopped right now, I'll still be a happy man because I was blessed to enjoy you for a little while. This moment right here, I've been waiting for since you made that phone call that brung you back into my life. Tiffany Jackson, I promised you that you'll be my wife before this week out. In front of my family and your parents will you make me the happiest man on earth and be my wife, before he could finish Tiffany was screaming yes Mike yes, I'll be your wife Mike pulled out the five-carat flawless princess cut he just scooped up about eight hours ago for sixty grand, Tiffany looked at the ring. Wow Mike wow and the two kissed. Michelle was standing by Tony and clapping with everybody else. When Tiffany pulled away from Mike she went over and embraced her parents still crying. Omar hugged Mike, Louis and Tony joined in. Felicia walked over to Tiffany and said welcome to the family and give her a hug. When Tony walked back over to Michelle, he pulled her close to him, maybe we can work at getting to that point in our lives. Caught by surprise the only thing she could say okay Tony. Michelle wrapped her arms around Tony's neck, I was a fool to treat you the way I treated you. Tony, you really hurt me, and I wanted you to feel what I felt. Michelle listens before you say anything else, we both need to leave the past in the past and let's start working on our future. I'm tired of being a fool, time to enjoy life, and that includes you and Keisha. When Mike was saying those words, bring back memories of the two of us. Michelle, I have thoughts of us all the time, you're the reason why I haven't settled down. When you left part of me left too. That's why we need to sit down and talk, we need to be really honesty with each other, I'm willing to put everything out there if you are. Baby tonight before Michelle could say anything else Mike and Tiffany walked over and introduced themselves to Michelle. Michelle commented on Tiffany ring, and she just glowed with happiness. Louis and Felicia were over by Omar helping him set the food out on the table. Everybody had forgotten about the dinner, so Omar called them to come sit and eat. Mike thanked everybody for coming and to enjoy the food. Shirley Tiffany's mom invited her new son-in-law to church Sunday morning something Mike was looking forward to. Shamekia and Diamond couldn't stop asking Tiffany all kinds of questions. Omar looked around the table to see his boys with smiles on their faces but was the faces that he was seeing real or fake. Mike no doubt but what about them other two. Only time would tell. After dinner Tiffany's parents said their goodbyes and they was the first ones to leave. Tiffany and Mike seemed to be in their own world. Mike whispered into Tiffany ear the night has just begun your chariot is here to pick you up. Shamekia and Mike had plan out a whole romantic night, with the limo picking them up from Omar and taking the downtown for a horse and carriage ride. Tiffany was very excited about what Mike had plan. After saying their goodbyes to everybody, they headed to the limo. Tiffany asked Mike, when did he have time to plan all this, he just said that he had a lot of help. Enjoying the full bar in the limo they finally arrived downtown. Riding the horse and carriage through the streets of downtown Atlanta with everybody looking when passing by was the icing on the cake to a wonderful evening. After riding through the city, we ended back in the limo on our way to the hotel. When they entered the lobby of the hotel, Tiffany was greeted with a dozen of red roses and then escorted to their room. Tiffany looked back at Mike who was smiling at her, putting his hand up to her lips and saying wait until we get in the room. When the bellboy opens the door to the room Tiffany couldn't believe her eyes, the room was cover with all kinds of beautiful flowers of all color. After the door close, Mike was all over Tiffany.

Tony and Michelle

After leaving Mike and Tiffany engagement dinner me and Michelle headed to my house to have that talk that was long overdue. Michelle was really ready for this talk with Tony, the way things ended between the two of them really didn't make sense to her. One minute everything was good and then she ended up doing her own thing, and Tony doing his. The ride was long and quiet from Omar house to Tony's. Michelle just stared out the window of the car, every now and then she would seek a peek at Tony, wondering what was he thinking about. She had called earlier to her parents' house to check on Keisha, but she got no answer, and she left a message letting them know that she'll pick her daughter up in the morning. Tony finally broke the silence, saying, after all these years you still avoid eye contact when you're nervous. Michelle just smiled and reached for Tony hand saying nothing. Your hands are so soft Michelle, just how I remembered them. Michelle finally spoke, you remembered those things about me all this time, I thought that you'll be forgotten about me. Never could forget about you lady, you were my first love. Never knew that Tony, why didn't you tell me? Never crossed my mind back then was too caught up in you and school. You were the good part of me, the part that didn't have a worry in the world. Before she could answer, I was pulling in my driveway, putting the car in park I quickly jump out of the car to open her door. Still the gentleman I see Michelle said anything and everything for you Tony answered. When Tony opens the door to the house, he turned to Michelle saying from this point of there's no turning back. Tony if you're ready I'm ready. Michelle does Keisha know that I'm her daddy. Tony, I told her about you a long time ago. After seeing you at the mall she really knew then and wanted to meet you. I wanted you to meet her a long time ago but, just couldn't build up the courage to face you after all these years. Do you hate me, Tony? Don't hate you just disappointed that you didn't have enough trust towards me to let me be there with you through all of this, but I must say you did your thing, being a career woman and a mom, I congratulate you on that. Thanks Tony but I had plenty help from my family and a few friends. So do your family know that I'm the father, my parents know. Tony my life is my life, don't care what people think. I know who you are and that's the only thing that should matter. I was happy that we run into each other at the mall. The person that I remembered would of knew off the rip that Kiesha was his daughter, and your actions didn't surprise me at all. I knew that if you see her that you would ask question. Looking in your eyes and seeing that it really hurt you, is making me realize that I made a costly mistake. Tony I'm truly sorry for my actions. Seeing you that day in the mall with my daughter changed a lot of wrongness in my life. For the first time in my life, I seen myself alone and it wasn't a good feeling. Now that I've got a chance to make my life, my life again, I'm not passing up that opportunity. Michelle, I want you and Keisha to be a big part of my life. It will take some time, but if we'll both willing to try we can't fail. Tony truth be told I never stop loving or dreaming about us being a family one day. That night when we talked and I let you know that I was pregnant, looking at your body demeanor made my decision for me. The way that you were laid back, hardly saying anything. Michelle, you've just told me you were pregnant with my child. I was just taking everything in that's all, but we can't undo the past, let's concentrate on the present and our future. Tony I've haven't trusted a man since you left or been without. After you everything was about my child and my career, but it's seems to me that you'll be the only man I'll ever trust. You made me tough as nails. Being focus was how I became one of the youngest judges in the district. Tony, will you do one thing for me, will you make love to me. Having Michelle ask me that question would have been music to my ears, so much had happened between us. In order for this to work I must truly forgive her and giving my all-in making love to her will be a start.

A Letter from
Mom

(Mike)

After a long night with Tiffany, the letter that my mom give Tiffany was on my mind. Ever since she gave me the letter, I've had it with me. While Tiffany was still asleep. I ease out of the bed and went in the other room to read the letter in private.

Hey Son,

If you're reading this letter, I'm gone on to a better place now. First, I just want to say that I'm so proud of you, even though it took some time to do so. Mike, you have your whole life ahead of you now and regardless of what anybody say it's never too late to live out your dreams. For thirty-something years I've watch you go through some difficult time, but you prevailed through it all. I watch you go from being lost in the world, then finding what your purpose in life is. Some people never get that second chance to make things right in their lives. You four guys have a lot of living ahead of you, but some changes and growing up has to be done if you guys want to continuing being friends. The world we live in changes every day; nothing remains the same Mike. When Omar lost Tosha, I watch closely as he put his life back together after he was broken down. When Omar really needed someone to talk to, he would stop by here and pour his heart out to me. Tony should have been there more for him, but he wasn't. Omar talked about you a lot. He said that the person you have become helped him out a lot. The phone conversation. And him coming to see you on the weekends was things he looked forward to. Omar's going to need you again Mike, even though his strong right now, he really hasn't time to let things really sink in. Be there for him son, because you're a brother to him in his eyes. Tiffany really a sweet girl, me and her have had some long talks about you, and just her hearing your name her face starts growing. The girl really loves you, so please don't mess things up son. Enjoy everything that God has plan for you Mike and never take your life or friends for granted. The guys are really going to need you to step up and to help them understand the true meaning of living. I love you son never forget that or me. My blessing is with all of you.

P.S. And I don't agree with Louis dating Felicia!!

Cheating (Louis)

On my way over to Felicia house after leaving Mike and Tiffany at Omar's, Nicole called and when I didn't answer she started texting me back-to-back saying that she needed to see me that it was very important that we meet up soon. Nicole had been on my mind all night for some reason, so I had to come up with a plan to ditch Felicia to see what Nicole wanted. When we arrived at Felicia, she went in first and I followed. We chilled and talked for a couple of hours. Felicia had fallen asleep on my chest, so I gently picked her up and carried her to the bedroom and laid her down in the bed. I told her that I needed to take care of some business and that I'll be back in the morning, she still was halfway asleep when she said OKAY. When I got in the car, picking up the phone and calling Nicole was the first thing that I did. She answered the phone saying it took you long enough. Where are you and are you coming over, she asked. I'm on my way now if you give me a little time, she said OKAY and hung up the phone. Nicole was still feeling some type of way about how Louis had been treating her ever since Felicia had come back into the picture. At one time she was Louis main chick now she hardly ever hears from him. She had come up with a plan to get Louis back and to hurt Felicia at the same time. When Louis reached Nicole apartment, the door was slightly open, and all the lights was off. Louis knocked and then pushed the door open, and there was Nicole butt-naked laying on the couch surrounded by candles with her legs wide open. With her hands she motions for Louis to come closer. Louis shut the door behind him and then locked it. Nicole had a big smile on her face and her plan seem to be working out just as she planned. Louis begins to undress but Nicole stopped him and asked him to make them a drink first so that they both could relax and enjoy each other. Louis hurried and fixed to strong mix drinks of grey goose and cranberry juice. Nicole fired up a laced blunt and give it to Louis. Louis never smoked a laced blunt before.

Nicole had Louis right where she wanted but then Louis begins to spit his game to Nicole. He grabbed Nicole and kissed her liked she dreamed about getting kissed and turned on at the same time by a man. She closed her eyes in begin to listen to what Louis was staying. Louis told Nicole that he was coming back to be with her, that he wanted her to have his child and to try to make a future together. Nicole was so caught up into what he was staying that she forgets to drop the pill into Louis drink. One thing Nicole did notice that Louis had did something he never did before, he slipped inside of Nicole without putting a condom on. That really made Nicole forget about her plans at the moment and just enjoy what was happening. Nicole asked Louis what he was trying to do to her, and he just answered let what's going to happen, and Nicole open her legs wider and invited Louis into her deeper. Having sex with Nicole was getting so good to Louis that he called Nicole Tiffany. Nicole didn't say a word, and the fire inside of her was lite again to get Louis back and hurt Tiffany. Nicole got up and fixed Louis another drink this time not forgetting to put the pill in. She climbed on top of Louis and rode him until the pill kicked and he fell asleep. Then she went into action with her plan. Her girlfriend Tab and sister Niecy was in the next room waiting all the time. While Louis was sleeping all three of the girls got naked and took all kinds of pictures of Louis. Every time they took a picture, they would send it to Felicia phone. All three of them did this over and over for hours. When Louis finally woke up Nicole and the other girls was gone. When Louis finally got his self together, he headed to his car thinking about how he dicked Nicole down all night. He looked on his windshield and there was an envelope with Louis name on it written in red lipstick. Louis opens the envelope and begin reading. Dear Louis. You just can't keep going around treating women any kind of way you want to, people have feelings. You're being a dog day are over. Louis you've run over me for the last time. When you get a chance go through your phone and always remember what goes around comes around. I'm just sorry another woman will end up hurt too.

Nicole

Louis grabbed his phone thirty miss calls from Omar, Mike and Felicia, he kept scrolling into he seen all the pictures and who they were sent to. Louis just sat in the car with his head down saying, how did I let this happen.

Felicia Mike and Omar

When Felicia receives the first picture, she thought it was someone playing on the phone until she took a closer look and seen Louis faces after a few pictures' tears begin to roll down her face and little did she know that Mike and Omar were receiving the same pictures. Felicia tried calling Louis phone but no answer. She begins to look at the pictures again, broken heart she forced herself to stop looking at the picture, she ran to the bathroom get in the corner of the shower and just let the tears flow. Omar was asleep when he received the first picture, he thought Louis was being funny, so he just ignores the first picture but after several more he had tried to call Louis to see what was going on. Omar looked at the pictures closely and said something isnt right. For a guy to be having a four-some, Louis looked like he was sleep. After looking at some more of the pictures I put the phone back on the charger and went to sleep. When I finally pulled myself from the shower, I called my girlfriend Shawn to come and sit with me. Because she was a good and true friend and wouldn't try to give me that I told you so speech. Louis still wasn't answering his phone, Nicole was one of the girls in the picture, but I didn't know the other two to me, Louis can't ever step feet in my presence again and I will let Mike know about this when I'm able to talk about it. When Shawn arrives at my place, I was still very emotional about the whole situation, so I just handed her the phone. She was speechless at first, just shaking her head, and then she looked up at me and said it's your choice to stay or leave, but you don't have to put up with this kind of bull. Did she really have the nerve to send you these pictures. Have you talk to Louis? I answered no and just started crying again. After reading my mom's letter I climbed back into bed with Tiffany and went to sleep. Early that morning the new phone Tiffany and Shamekia had gotten for me was making a beeping noise over and over.

So, me not knowing how to really work the phone I ask Tiffany to show me how to do it. She said that I have ten pictures sent from Louis phone, and when she opens the first picture, she looked at me and gave me the phone. Looking at the picture on the phone, I reached and pulled Tiffany to me letting her know that I have no idea about what Louis got going on. Felicia was the first thought that came to my mine. Louis told me that he was really ready to settle down with my cousin and now this. Tiffany was still looking at me crazy, let's call Louis and get to the bottom of this.

Louis didn't answer the phone, so I called Omar to see have he heard from him. When Omar picked up the phone before I could say anything, Omar laughing through the phone saying, I already ready know bro, what the world is on Louis mind. Remember him saying that he was done messing around on Felicia with that Nicole chick. Omar, Louis really tripping this time, we just had a talk with him the other night, and don't forget about the incident at Felicia place the other day with the flat tires. But Mike looks a little closer at the pictures. On every one of them Louis is sleep, with all that going on, who can you sleep, Omar asked. Maybe it's more to this then we think. We just need to find Louis to see what's going on. Have you called to see if he's at Felicia sleep? I've haven't called her yet, but I will, and I'll call you back. So, after hanging up with Omar I called Felicia, when she answered the phone, the way she sounded explained it all. I asked Felicia what's going on and she just starting yelling in the phone about the pictures of Louis and the girls. Louis had really messed up this time. Trying to calm Felicia down wasn't an easy task, she kept asking me where the hell Louis was. I explain to her what me and Omar talked about. That calm her now for a minute, but she still was very upset. I told her that me and Omar would be over her house in a couple of hours and hung up the phone. Before calling Omar back Tiffany asked me why would Louis do Felicia like this and left out the room. Walking behind her and grabbing her by the wrist and pulling her close to me, letting her know that this doesn't have anything to do with me. Louis really had some explaining to do. Tiffany just kept shaking her head saying it's not right Mike any way you put it. Period. Trying to tell her its two sides to every story wasn't working. I picked up the phone to call Omar back, but he didn't answer the phone. After waiting a few minutes, I called again, Omar answered saying Louis was in a car accident and on his way to the hospital. Omar hurried and gave me all the information and hung up. Tiffany looked at me and asked what is going on, we put our clothes on and left for the hospital. After dropping the girls off at the aunt's house, I headed to the hospital. The paramedics said that Louis had fainted while driving and run off the road and hit a tree. He was unconscious and not responding, they found his phone on the floorboard of his car and my number was the first one on the call log, so that's how they got my number. When I reached the hospital, I thought about the time when Tosha was here, memories I didn't want to think about. When the nurse told me that Louis was in surgery, that when it hit me, this could be serious. So much had happen that I forgot to call Tony to let him know what was going on. Didn't want to talk on the phone in the hospital so I sent him a text, letting him know about all what happen. After about fifteen minutes he replied saying he was on his way. Mike and Tiffany had arrived, and Mike was telling me about the conversation he had with his cousin Felicia. What his was saying was something you hear about happening to someone else not your close homeboy. Tiffany didn't really say much she just listens mostly. When the nurse finally got around to talking to us, we found out that they found cocaine and some date rape drugs that man use on women in his blood stream. Louis had a broken arm and thirty stitches over the right eye, now Mike said it was time to call Felicia. Louis was sleep through all that was going on. Nicole and her friends must have had this planned out to get back at Louis. When Mike called and told Felicia what the nurse said, she couldn't believe what she was hearing. Nicole would go through all this just to get back at Louis. The nurse explained and asked some questions about who Louis was with last night, but no one said a word. She said that Louis would probably be out until tomorrow, so we just sat around and waited on Tony and Felicia. Me and Mike didn't say another word about Louis or the pictures until we talk to Louis.

Louis and the Guys

Waking up in the hospital, trying to remember the events that led me to being here. Looking around the room trying to adjust my eyes and there she was Felicia, the one person that I wasn't ready for yet. Before I could say anything, she got up and walked over to me. What was you thinking she asked? This girl has really messed things up for you this time. All the guys received the same pictures I did and they're outside in the waiting room, worried about you Louis. It's time to stop with playing games with people emotions. I'm very disappointed that you put yourself in a position like this. You're lucky this time, Louis she really could have made things bad for you. Why was you even there? Felicia, there's no excuse I can give you right now. I really don't know what I was thinking. Sorry for embarrassing and hurting you. Nicole finally got me back and hurt you in the process. Louis for right now just please stay away from me, I've taken enough of your lying and cheating ass, I refuse to be your doormat, goodbye Louis. Please let me explain Felicia, what's to explain Louis, you were at her house, remember you left me at home sleep, without saying anything else she walked out. When Felicia left out, I really didn't feel anything, didn't know if it was the drugs or just me truly not having feelings for her. She said that Nicole sent the guys the same pictures, that means Mike know I played his cousin. Taking deep breathes breathing the guys walked in. Damn Louis Omar said, you really got yourself into a mess this time. How are you feeling? I'm okay just a little sore Omar and confused about somethings. Louis how could you let your guard down with this girl, knowing that she's out for blood Tony asked? To be honest Tony really didn't think Nicole would take it this far after flatting my tires, really underestimated her. I turned towards Mike way, waiting on him to say something, but he didn't. You know that she drugged you and you had a delayed reaction while you were driving and had an accident that's why you're her Omar said walking over to me. Your car is total and by now you're probably all over the internet. Louis why didn't you cut that girl off like you said you was, Mike asked. Again, you put my cousin at risk again, after I asked was you real with her, and you said that Felicia was your future, Louis I feel like you played me like a fool. It doesn't make no sense who you just continue to run over females. Yea we did its years ago, when we were young, but we're grown men now. What if some guy treated Shamekia and Diamond like that? What would you do? Louis I know that I'm one not to preach because of my track record with women, but when you've had time to think and when you have gone through some things, your whole outlook on things is different. You ever wondered why women sometimes treat us unfair because it's men like you that has broken them down where, they can't trust or love anymore. Women turning to other women for love and affection that we're supposed to give them, but we're too busy giving to them and everybody else. Mike's right Louis Omar jumping in, now Mike has to go and sit down and talk to Felicia, his own flesh and blood about what one of his best friends did to her, can't even imagine how that's going to turn out. Look Louis Tony explaining we've all needed to do some growing up and it's been long overdue, we've been covering up for each other since grade school and it was fun then, but we're grown man now. This girl could have killed you and hurt Felicia and who's to say that she's finish Louis. Something should have made us stop this a long time ago, when we watched Omar almost lose his mind when Tosha died. Instead of us being there for him as a true brother should, we were so caught up with trying to sleep with every girl we could and left Omar out in the cold. Not a day goes by. Omar that I don't beat myself up for that. Mike, we did you wrong too, we acted like you wasn't there and I myself am truly sorry. Since you've been back Mike, something inside of me wants change. It's bad that it takes something like this had to happen for us to open our eyes. Every day the sunrise and we lose a little self, and we gain a little self some for the good and some for the bad. Every day is different from the next, that's why we must change also, or we'll be doing the same thing years from now. That's true what you're saying Tony, Mike interrupted, but actions speak louder than words. Change isn't a one-day thing, it takes time sacrifices and patience. Change starts within a person and it's something they want to do; nobody can make a person change. Louis really wanted to talk to Mike by himself but by the look on Mike face, maybe it would be better later. What are we as men willing to change, Mike asked? Finally, Omar said something Louis we're going to let you get some rest, but you really need to make up your mind on how you're going to handle this. I don't know what you did to this lady, but she's out of control. Maybe it's time to really cut her loose because I have a gut feeling you're still fooling around or leading this girl on Louis. And you can really make things go a little better with Felicia if you tell her the truth, you owe her that much Louis. She been putting up with your bullshit long enough. If you're not serious about her let her, go, because eventually you and Mike will clash. That's his cousin and you really did some disrespectful shit. Tony you're a lawyer what can be done to Nicole for drugging Louis. Criminal charges could be brought up on her if Louis press the issue Tony responded. So, the balls in your corner Louis, you keep playing games with Nicole until someone really gets hurt or we stop this now, asked Omar. At one point me and Nicole was cool, and I could have seen something serious between us, did my actions make her act like that I don't know, but before Felicia or anybody get hurt, I'll do whatever it takes to stop Nicole. Fellas, maybe some of the crazy things we did in the past is catching up with us, Omar mumbled, have you ever thought about that our actions created in life would determine our future. Like if people knew that smoking cigarettes after a long period of time would hurt them later in life keep smoking. That's why I try to do the right things now, because it's not my future anymore but it's Shamekia and Diamond also. Louis you get some rest now we've bothered you enough, but we'll be back to close the chapter on this Nicole chick. Mike just looked at Louis and walked off. The guys said goodbye and the left Louis thinking, could he really go through with having charges filed against Nicole.

Mike and Felicia

Me and Tiffany rode around for hours looking for Felicia, when she wouldn't answer the phone. Then something told me to ride by the old park in the old neighborhood and there she was sitting on the merry go round all by herself. When we were young, that was the one place we called our own private space. She looked up at me with tears in her eyes telling me you said you've always had me back, how did you let this happen, you've always protected me from guys like Louis. When we were kids, you promised that you'll never leave me to defend for myself. You were the one who made it possible for me to go to college, you took money out your own pocket, Mike you were a good person back then, even better now. Sitting down beside her with Tiffany right by myside, remember when we use to talk about leaving Georgia and moving to New York to make movies. You would be my leading actor and I would be the director. Dreams we had of becoming big, but when we really got the nerves up to do it, our moms get wind of it and talked us out of it. It was me and you against the world,

Bonny and Clyde. She looked up at me with a smile on her face washing away the tears. You always knew how to make me smile and forget about what I'm going through Mike. Not trying to make you forget just here to let you know, that's life not over and you'll make it through. It just hurts so bad right now. Remember the day before I had to turn myself in, how you talked me into going to the party that the guys were having for me. You let me know that you'll be here when no one else will, to me you save me from running away that night. Around you my true self comes out and I cried on your shoulder that night because I wasn't ready to go to prison. We were here sitting on this same merry go around but things were the other way around you were talking to me. Felicia, God has been working with me when I was at my lowest. He gives me strength beyond my ability. You got to start making Felicia happy. It's up to you to find out who you really are. Times like this is when I get on my knees and pray now. God help me make it through those seven years in prison. I can tell you this and that but only God knows the answer to what you're looking for. Mike, you have change so much over these last couple of years, because the Mike I know would of tore Louis head up. Before your mom passed away, she said that you would be a change person when you came home. The letters she got from you every week was her therapy and kept her around a little longer. Your words gave her strength. Mike, I knew Aunt Louise didn't agree with me dating Louis, things just happen so fast. Felicia you're smart enough to figure this out on your own, sometimes the very things we want aren't the things we need. After following Felicia home, Tiffany finally said something after being quiet the whole day. Mike, I listen to you very closely today, the way that you handle things with Felicia showed me a gentler side of you. When you were away, I remember you telling me that your outlook about certain life situations were different now. Just hearing you speak now, makes me see the change in you. If you would have asked me seven years ago, where would I be, I'll never guessed being right here with you. Last night was excepted, you having my parents there really touched me and it showed me the respect you have for me. I'm still walking on cloud nine Mike thank you baby. But the more I think about Felicia the less I feel sorry for Louis and that's bad feeling that way towards him. The only thing a women ask from men now is to be just honest and faithful. We make our own money now and we're not looking for any handouts. It's a new century and some men need to come to grips and get with the program. Tiffany this thing about Louis really has you pissed off. But always keep in mind baby, that's Felicia's a grown woman, she knew what type of guy Louis was, but she hung around praying and wishing for him to change, it's just up to that person to want to change. Enough about them Tiffany, let's go home and enjoy each other.

Tony's Past

After leaving the hospital, I just wanted to go home call Michelle and spend some time with her and Keisha. Over the last few days, a lot has happened since Mike been home. Finding out that I had a daughter was a blessing for me. She was that reason I was looking for to turn my life around. All the different women I've dated over the years never gave me a reason to want to change. If things would have turned out different for me and Michelle back in college, there's no telling where I would be. Sleeping with Michelle again wasn't something I wanted to do, but when you're in the heat of passion, all self-controlled is threw out the window. It's been a long time waking up beside a lady and not rushing to leave. Before calling Michelle my phone rung and to my surprise Denise was calling, haven't heard or talked to her in a couple of days. Answering the phone, I could hear the tension in her voice. Tony, you can't call me and let me know that you're okay she asked me. Maybe I could come be and spend some me and you time. Tonight, not a good night for me, I've already made plans answering her back. So, when you're not busy Tony gave me a call because you need to come and scratch this itch I have she responded. Saying okay and hanging up Michelle face came in my head. Being with Michelle has made me forget about the other women that's in my life. For the last couple of days building a family is all I've been thinking about. Giving my daughter something, I didn't have, a home with two loving parent. My mom did what she could with me for so long, I thank God that my Uncle Red was around to keep me in check. It was his influence and work ethics that made me strive harder to make something out of myself. When the guys were out hanging and doing they thing, Uncle Red had me out working if I wasn't studying. Red died my last year of college, but I know in my heart that he was proud of me. Didn't meet my daddy until Red's funeral, didn't have anything to say to him then, and don't have nothing to say to him now. The resentment I feel for my father is a feeling I wouldn't want no child to feel. It's a feeling that haunts you every so often. Maybe one day the feeling may leave me, but if not it's something I've learn to live with. I'm so glad that I'll have a chance to be in Keisha's life. To show her the love that was shown to me by Red. Just thinking about Louis situation, I have to be up front with Denise and Michelle because I refuse to lose my daughter. After checking in with my secretary Cindy I called Michelle. Cindy was an old high school friend who I kept in touch with through college, she was a big sister to me. When I first started my business, she help me put everything in order. Through the years she seen me go through a lot of drama with different women never judging me. Michelle answered the phone on the first ring sounding excited what's up Tony she asked, just calling to see when can I come over? Now isn't a good time, things are happening so fast between us. What are you trying to say Michelle, last night it was us starting all over again? What change since last night. Tony, I've got to think this all the way through, if I choose us, you have to be all in with us. You have to realize that I'm a judge and if you'll done anything wrong in your past that would embarrass me or make me look bad, I really need to know. Okay Michelle, I'll tell you everything and you must do the same and what I tell you stays between us, do you want me to come over or you coming to me Michelle. Come to me she answered. Telling Michelle all about Omar and Mike, this thing with Louis and about my dating in the past was all the things that could do damage to me and Michelle. She told me that Keisha would be there, and we could start getting to know each other. Wasn't too worried about the dating, but Mike taking the charges for Omar and doing all that time and Louis and Nicole drama. Michelle got to come clear too, after all these years, she's no saint. Thinking about my past, me and the guys made a promise never to tell what really went down that night between Omar and Tosha's ex. That's part of my life that will stay between me and boys. Michelle will have to deal with it, if it ever comes up. When I pulled in Michelle's yard, a tall dark skin guy was leaving. What's up I asked Michelle. She answered, we really need to talk. Tony when we went our separate ways in college, I started dating Travis during my pregnancy. He knew he wasn't the father but vowed to be there for me if I needed anything. Well, he's been in Keisha's life since she been born. Now that you've entered the picture, I had to tell Travis and he didn't take it very well. He threatens to take me to court. Why would he threaten you like that if he knew you was already pregnant when he first met you Michelle, somethings not adding up. Who last name does Keisha have and has Travis sign any papers dealing with Keisha. No Tony, I'm not dirty like that and he knew all about you because I told him everything. Well, why is he mad because you told him that I was back in the picture. Tony, he thought that he could have a relationship with me, but I never liked him like that. We only sleep together a few times and then I just throw myself into my career and just left him alone. I was afraid this would happen. When you called earlier and I said this wasn't a good time, he was here then. He wouldn't leave until you showed up. For a judge you couldn't just call the police and have him removed from your house, Michelle. Not trying to do all that Tony remember I'm a high-profile person, dont need no one digging all in my past. Michelle, you know he's not going away, so you may have to go public, because I'm not going to let another man raise my daughter. Just let me talk to him and try to make him understand. What makes you think he will understand, he feels like he's been played by you. Damn Tony, you're supposed to be on my side, where's all of this coming from? Because Michelle, you shut me out of my daughter's life and let another man in her life, knowing he wasn't the father, what do you except from me. Tell me something Michelle, if I didn't see you and Keisha that day, would you ever have found me and told me. Michelle walked out the room and return with a stack of folders all with my name on them dated back to when I was in college. She handed me the folders with tears in her eyes, Tony I've been keeping up with you every day since we broke up, the answer to your question, yes, I going to tell you, but every time I got up the nerve I'll see you at some restaurants with a different woman, and it wasn't one time but several times. You weren't ready to hear about me having your daughter, you were having too much fun. That night with Omar, and Mike taking the charge, I wanted to help so bad, I never seen you cry, until you broke down at Omar's wife funeral when they brung Mike in handcuffed, Tony it took everything not to show my face. So, Michelle, you are telling me you've been around all this time haven't said nothing. Tony, I didn't know how to come at you, the way I ended things with you, made me wonder, how were you going to react to me. See you all those different times with those different women just made it harder for me. Omar seen me a couple of times passing with Keisha, but he really wasn't paying attention. It impresses me to see you build your law firm from the ground up and what it has become now. I've been beating myself up year after year about the decision I made that night in the college dorm. Tony if I could take it all back, I would do everything different, and we wouldn't be here having this conversation. My first couple of years after Keisha was born, were rough for me. I cried a lot, even though my family was there, I still felt so alone without you. Looking at Keisha and seeing you made me regret everything I did. Several times I dialed your number just to hear your voice. Tony I was so caught up in my feelings toward how things could have been between us that I almost lost myself but forgetting about you was out of the question. That's when I started tracking you down, it maybe sounds crazy to you, but it keeps me from losing my mine. Michelle you should of just came to me and we could have talked about it. I've always wondered where did you run off to. After you left college, people told me you went back home to your family. I called a million times to your house and your mom and dad would answer the phone saying you're not there with an attitude. Michelle let's just leave the past in the past and start building a future together. We both have made mistakes, that we have learned from. You already know everything about me almost. Michelle, I have some loose ends to tie up too. Never had to tell a lady that I'm dedicating my life to one person, well two in this matter and starting a family. Michelle looked up at me, I could tell she wanted to ask some questions, but she just played it off by saying, make it quick because she don't share. She kissed me and asked me was I ready, and I said ready for what, to meet your daughter Tony.

The Guys (Omar)

Louis was being release from the hospital and me and the guys was going to pick him. Mike had called me that night asking me if I've heard from Tony. I let Mike know that Tony was spending time with Michelle and getting to know his daughter Keisha. These last few days Tony had really stepped up to the plate. He called every lady friend he was dealing with and told them about Michelle and Keisha. Tony said that everything went smooth, and it wasn't any hard feelings between them. Tony had taken a leave of absent from his business, the few clients he did have understood and Cindy put all the new clients on hold for now until Tony returned. Keisha wasn't coming around and talking at first, but eventually she came around and now you can't keep the two of them apart. Tony and Michelle agreed that Tony could sign the birth certificate when he was ready. Louis hadn't heard from Felicia, but after filing charges and having Nicole and her friends locked up for drugging him, she'd been calling leaving all kinds of threats on his phone. I was headed to pick up Mike first. He was at home by himself, Tiffany had to go in to make arrangements to move to a bigger shop. The building she was renting wasn't big enough to accommodate all the new plans she had for her salon. Her and Mike are making moves together and enjoying each other every step of the way. Tiffany is good for Mike; she reminds me of Tosha a little. Tosha never judged no one out publicly. I could tell Tiffany wanted to say something to Louis, but she didn't. But when we left the two of them together alone while we talked to the doctor, Louis told us Tiffany had some words with him, she said, that being new to everybody she wouldn't judge or criticize anyone, but she's in Mike's life and she's not going anywhere. She explained to Louis that he really hurt Mike with his lies. She also told Louis, but at the end of the day, he blamed himself for teaching you all that slick stuff to get females. When Tiffany finish with Louis, she made it known to him, to keep that mess away from her home and man. Mike was looking out the window with I pulled into Tiffany driveway, Mike had been staying with her since he came home from prison. Mike still had his mom's house but, he was hesitating to go to his mom's house. That was something I plan to talk to him about. Since him and Tiffany was planning on buying a new house. Mike eased into the front seat looking at me and smiling saying, it's sure is nice to be at home with the ones you love. I wanted to ask him why was he so happy today. But I'll just wait until he tells me. So, what's up Mike, enjoying everything that God is blessing me with Omar. Where are my two-pretty princess at today bro. They're spending the week with grandma, and granddad. All they talking about is, helping Tiffany plan the wedding. Since Tosha's death the girls have never really gotten close to other women besides their, grandma and aunt. But they really like Tiffany. And I truly believe Tiffany will be good for the girls. Omar, I never really asked you this, but it's just me and you right now, how are you really doing. Over the years Mike I learned to live with whatever life throws at me. When you were locked up and Tosha started getting sick, I really looked back over my life and ask God to forgive me for all the wrong I did, because in my mind his was punishing me. Every day comes with a new challenge for me. To me, my life is all about family and not taking a second of life for granted. Sure, I hurt and still cry, half of me died with Tosha, but having you around again gives me something to smile about. I can't say this enough, but I'm really grateful for what you did. I know that you gave seven years of your life for me and my family. Before Tosha died, she made me promise to always have your back no matter what, if you're wrong or right. We cool Omar you stood up and did what you said you would do; you took care of your family and me.

If I had to do it all over again I would, so stop feeling like you owe me, taking that charge for you save me, and made me the man I'm today. Remember this Omar if you don't remember nothing else God don't make mistakes. Pulling into Tony's yard, he's already standing in the driveway talking to Michelle. Tony walks over to the car with Michelle and tells me and Mike that he wants us to meet somebody special to him and calls his daughter Keisha over to meet us. Never thought the day that I would see Tony being a dad, but life has all kinds of surprises. Keisha looked just like Tony when his was younger, and she had his smile. She was a little shy a first, but she opened up to me and Mike. Tony said his goodbyes and kissed both of them and jumped in the car with us. Tony was smiling from head to toe. What's up Mike asked Tony, I have to tell you guys something Tony replied I've just finished the paperwork's, Keisha had my last name, she's really mine, the blood test came back showing she's the same blood type as I am. At first, I'm not going to lie, I had my doubts about Keisha being mines, but as I begin to wonder Michelle wasn't that kind of person to go around lying like that. Since I've known her, she never tried to pull anything over on me when I seen them that day in the mall seeing that little girl did something to me. She's really mines Omar, can you guys believe that I have a daughter. But Tony let me ask you this Mike said.

So, what are you going to do about your living arrangements? I'm going to rent my house out and moving in with Michelle and Keisha. Those are some big steps; Tony are you really ready for that. Yes Omar, I'm tired of the club scene tired of women that just want to have fun. I'm ready to settle down, I want to take vacations with my family. My business is good, it's time for a change in my life guys, can't keep doing the same old thing. Every day that goes by is a day I wasted and can't get back who are you and what have you done with Tony Omar asked laughing. These last few days, I've really enjoyed, Michelle is good for me, she makes me feel like a different man. She's not one of those women that needs a man to define them. She's her own person and that makes me want her even more. Glad to hear and see that your happy bro Mike said. Not meaning to change the subject, but I seem something on the news the other day and it's really been bothering me. What is it Omar, Tony asked? What's up with all these police killings, can't something be done to stop this. Omar, I've seen it too, when I was in prison watching the news was a must. Listening to the guys in there, you could feel the tension. In the air. It wasn't a black or white thing, just men fed up period. Our children are not safe to walk in their own neighborhood anymore. When my mom and her generation was going up, they had people like Martin Luther King and Malcom X, even though we have a black president we really need our other black leaders to step up. You have more preachers stepping up them leaders. I totally agree with you Mike Tony said. I'm a lawyer and I see a lot of wrong done to people firsthand. In order for something to change, sorry to say, but we have to change ourselves. First, we have to get the authority back to raise our own kids. Most kids these days come home every day to an empty house, because mom and dad is out there working trying to make a living, so now the T.V. and computer are teaching our kids instead of us. If you go or drive by a park in the afternoon the basketball courts and playgrounds are empty. Back in the days when we were going up, you couldn't keep us from the courts or being outside period. Things have really changed guys. Omar being a single parent of two girls is hard. Yes, Tony it's hard if you make it, me and my girls have a understand that if something wrong we talk about it. We don't go and run to outsiders with our problems. Second, I'm their father no one else, what I say goes. I'm their daddy and I don't try to be their best friend. Tony you and Mike will be asking me all kind of questions, you have a daughter and Mike and Tiffany working on theirs. Eventually certain circumstances will come about but just always remember that you are the parent and they're the child. If parents were to be parents again and stop letting social media raise their kids maybe things would change. God has been taken out of a lot of things and replaced with man ideas explained Mike. The world we live in is about everything right then and now. We want everything to be instant, but life doesn't work like that. In order to appreciate life's blessing more, we may need to understand what the blessing is. Everything is being taken for granted including people. Relationship are not relationship, because people feel like that don't have to work at it. People just don't realize that the way you got that person is the way you have to keep them, but now a day when we get that special someone the romancing leaved. I forgot to ask you Mike, Omar said, how's Felicia doing, and how did the talk you had with her go, Omar Felicia's a grown woman, who knew what she was dealing with from the start. This wasn't the first time Louis cheated on her. Felicia has some soul searching to do for herself. She understands that some people just not going to change. Last time we talked to her, and a couple of her friends were headed towards Florida to get away for a few days. Have Louis tried to get in touch with her Tony asked? I don't know Tony she didn't say anything about it, if he did. It's more things we need to catch up on guys maybe one day we can all just sit down over a few beers and just talk Mike asked. Tony and Omar agreed to sitting down and talking. The guys had finally arrived at the hospital to pick up Louis, but as they were headed into the hospital entrance Mike spotted Louis in a car leaving with Nicole.

The Guys (Omar)

Louis was being release from the hospital and me and the guys was going to pick him. Mike had called me that night asking me if I've heard from Tony. I let Mike know that Tony was spending time with Michelle and getting to know his daughter Keisha. These last few days Tony had really stepped up to the plate. He called every lady friend he was dealing with and told them about Michelle and Keisha. Tony said that everything went smooth, and it wasn't any hard feelings between them. Tony had taken a leave of absent from his business, the few clients he did have understood and Cindy put all the new clients on hold for now until Tony returned. Keisha wasn't coming around and talking at first, but eventually she came around and now you can't keep the two of them apart. Tony and Michelle agreed that Tony could sign the birth certificate when he was ready. Louis hadn't heard from Felicia, but after filing charges and having Nicole and her friends locked up for drugging him, she'd been calling leaving all kinds of threats on his phone. I was headed to pick up Mike first. He was at home by himself, Tiffany had to go in to make arrangements to move to a bigger shop. The building she was renting wasn't big enough to accommodate all the new plans she had for her salon. Her and Mike are making moves together and enjoying each other every step of the way. Tiffany is good for Mike; she reminds me of Tosha a little. Tosha never judged no one out publicly. I could tell Tiffany wanted to say something to Louis, but she didn't. But when we left the two of them together alone while we talked to the doctor, Louis told us Tiffany had some words with him, she said, that being new to everybody she wouldn't judge or criticize anyone, but she's in Mike's life and she's not going anywhere. She explained to Louis that he really hurt Mike with his lies. She also told Louis, but at the end of the day, he blamed himself for teaching you all that slick stuff to get females. When Tiffany finish with Louis, she made it known to him, to keep that mess away from her home and man. Mike was looking out the window with I pulled into Tiffany driveway, Mike had been staying with her since he came home from prison. Mike still had his mom's house but, he was hesitating to go to his mom's house. That was something I plan to talk to him about. Since him and Tiffany was planning on buying a new house. Mike eased into the front seat looking at me and smiling saying, it's sure is nice to be at home with the ones you love. I wanted to ask him why was he so happy today. But I'll just wait until he tells me. So, what's up Mike, enjoying everything that God is blessing me with Omar. Where are my two-pretty princess at today bro. They're spending the week with grandma, and granddad. All they talking about is, helping Tiffany plan the wedding. Since Tosha's death the girls have never really gotten close to other women besides their, grandma and aunt. But they really like Tiffany. And I truly believe Tiffany will be good for the girls. Omar, I never really asked you this, but it's just me and you right now, how are you really doing. Over the years Mike I learned to live with whatever life throws at me. When you were locked up and Tosha started getting sick, I really looked back over my life and ask God to forgive me for all the wrong I did, because in my mind his was punishing me. Every day comes with a new challenge for me. To me, my life is all about family and not taking a second of life for granted. Sure, I hurt and still cry, half of me died with Tosha, but having you around again gives me something to smile about. I can't say this enough, but I'm really grateful for what you did. I know that you gave seven years of your life for me and my family. Before Tosha died, she made me promise to always have your back no matter what, if you're wrong or right. We cool Omar you stood up and did what you said you would do; you took care of your family and me.

If I had to do it all over again I would, so stop feeling like you owe me, taking that charge for you save me, and made me the man I'm today. Remember this Omar if you don't remember nothing else God don't make mistakes. Pulling into Tony's yard, he's already standing in the driveway talking to Michelle. Tony walks over to the car with Michelle and tells me and Mike that he wants us to meet somebody special to him and calls his daughter Keisha over to meet us. Never thought the day that I would see Tony being a dad, but life has all kinds of surprises. Keisha looked just like Tony when his was younger, and she had his smile. She was a little shy a first, but she opened up to me and Mike. Tony said his goodbyes and kissed both of them and jumped in the car with us. Tony was smiling from head to toe. What's up Mike asked Tony, I have to tell you guys something Tony replied I've just finished the paperwork's, Keisha had my last name, she's really mine, the blood test came back showing she's the same blood type as I am. At first, I'm not going to lie, I had my doubts about Keisha being mines, but as I begin to wonder Michelle wasn't that kind of person to go around lying like that. Since I've known her, she never tried to pull anything over on me when I seen them that day in the mall seeing that little girl did something to me. She's really mines Omar, can you guys believe that I have a daughter. But Tony let me ask you this Mike said. So, what are you going to do about your living arrangements? I'm going to rent my house out and moving in with Michelle and Keisha. Those are some big steps; Tony are you really ready for that. Yes Omar, I'm tired of the club scene tired of women that just want to have fun. I'm ready to settle down, I want to take vacations with my family. My business is good, it's time for a change in my life guys, can't keep doing the same old thing. Every day that goes by is a day I wasted and can't get back who are you and what have you done with Tony Omar asked laughing. These last few days, I've really enjoyed, Michelle is good for me, she makes me feel like a different man. She's not one of those women that needs a man to define them. She's her own person and that makes me want her even more. Glad to hear and see that your happy bro Mike said. Not meaning to change the subject, but I seem something on the news the other day and it's really been bothering me. What is it Omar, Tony asked? What's up with all these police killings, can't something be done to stop this. Omar, I've seen it too, when I was in prison watching the news was a must. Listening to the guys in there, you could feel the tension. In the air. It wasn't a black or white thing, just men fed up period. Our children are not safe to walk in their own neighborhood anymore. When my mom and her generation was going up, they had people like Martin Luther King and Malcom X, even though we have a black president we really need our other black leaders to step up. You have more preachers stepping up them leaders. I totally agree with you Mike Tony said. I'm a lawyer and I see a lot of wrong done to people firsthand. In order for something to change, sorry to say, but we have to change ourselves. First, we have to get the authority back to raise our own kids. Most kids these days come home every day to an empty house, because mom and dad is out there working trying to make a living, so now the T.V. and computer are teaching our kids instead of us. If you go or drive by a park in the afternoon the basketball courts and playgrounds are empty. Back in the days when we were going up, you couldn't keep us from the courts or being outside period. Things have really changed guys. Omar being a single parent of two girls is hard. Yes, Tony it's hard if you make it, me and my girls have a understand that if something wrong we talk about it. We don't go and run to outsiders with our problems. Second, I'm their father no one else, what I say goes. I'm their daddy and I don't try to be their best friend. Tony you and Mike will be asking me all kind of questions, you have a daughter and Mike and Tiffany working on theirs. Eventually certain circumstances will come about but just always remember that you are the parent and they're the child. If parents were to be parents again and stop letting social media raise their kids maybe things would change. God has been taken out of a lot of things and replaced with man ideas explained Mike. The world we live in is about everything right then and now. We want everything to be instant, but life doesn't work like that. In order to appreciate life's blessing more, we may need to understand what the blessing is. Everything is being taken for granted including people. Relationship are not relationship, because people feel like that don't have to work at it. People just don't realize that the way you got that person is the way you have to keep them, but now a day when we get that special someone the romancing leaved. I forgot to ask you Mike, Omar said, how's Felicia doing, and how did the talk you had with her go, Omar Felicia's a grown woman, who knew what she was dealing with from the start. This wasn't the first time Louis cheated on her. Felicia has some soul searching to do for herself. She understands that some people just not going to change. Last time we talked to her, and a couple of her friends were headed towards Florida to get away for a few days. Have Louis tried to get in touch with her Tony asked? I don't know Tony she didn't say anything about it, if he did. It's more things we need to catch up on guys maybe one day we can all just sit down over a few beers and just talk Mike asked. Tony and Omar agreed to sitting down and talking. The guys had finally arrived at the hospital to pick up Louis, but as they were headed into the hospital entrance Mike spotted Louis in a car leaving with Nicole.

Three Months Later
Omar and Mike

Been putting off about going to pack up things at my mom's house since I've been out. Every time I'm on my way to do it something comes up. These last few months with Tiffany have been very busy. Making plans for the wedding, moving into the new salon and moving into the new house as well. Didn't expected to come home and do all of this at one time. I've got to admit, things between me and Tiffany heated up fast. Being with her now is different with any other female. Never thought a female would have me the way she has me. There's no secrets between us and the past is just the past. Our future is what we're counting on and we're the only people that can come between us. Being truly in in love with someone will have you doing things and going places you never thought you would do. Never sat in a beauty or nail salon waiting for a girl. To get finished. Every day that goes by I try to treat Tiffany like it's my last day on earth with her. Sometimes she hugs me and start crying, saying you loving me the way you do, touches the deepest part of my soul. No man has ever made me feel like this. Only if she knew what's in store for her. I plan to share every moment I could with her, because tomorrow is promise to no one, and I've wasted to much of my time on what ifs. A true man doesn't rely on what ifs but say what he's going to do and make it happen. I can't see myself without Tiffany, at this stage in my life. She been what I needed to make me a better person. God plays a big part in who I'm now. He put the pieces to the puzzle together forty-two years ago. This morning when Tiffany left to go to work, I caught myself standing in the window daydreaming about the last couple of nights making love to her. Today is the day that I handle things at my mom's house and Omar is riding with me, Tony had to work, and Louis been missing in action ever since he left the hospital with Nicole. He wont answer or return no of our phone calls. Really don't know what to think or say about Louis but lives too short for games. Pulling in Omar driveway I see Diamond playing in the front yard and when she's seen me, she runs to the car all smiles and hugs. Hey Uncle Mike, where's Tiffany, can't wait to be in the wedding sounding all excited. Tiffany at work Diamond and how are you doing little lady. Nothing just doing little girl stuff and trying to stay out of Shamekia's way. How about me and you ride to the ice cream parlor and sit down and talk, go ask your dad. Being the baby of the family, sometimes you need a little more extra attention. She came back out the house running and ready to go, Omar behind her be back in an hour Omar. Me and Diamond ate ice cream cones, and she talked my head off, didn't know a five-year-old could talk and ask so many questions. When we return Diamond hug me and yawn then went in the house. Omar jumped in the car laughing and saying she's a hand full isn't she. Diamond has so much energy and life in her, no worries just taken life in. That's how lives supposed to be, but we put pressure on ourselves when we try to do too much instead of just letting things be, now a days we get in the way too much. Our lives didn't have to be stressed out all the time, we as individual just have to learn to take each day as it comes. I plan on living a long and prosperous life, enjoy the little things that so many people take for granted, like enjoying a cool breeze on a hot summer day. Mike that sounds good but everyday not going to be peaches and cream, just because I smile and go about my business doesn't mean that everything always good. Being a single dad isn't easy and some days I just want to give up, then I hear Tosha voice whisper in my ear, that's not what you promised me. Not a day goes by that I don't think about her Mike. If I didn't have memories of her in my mind, I've may have lost it a long time ago. Let me ask you something personal Omar, do you think that you'll ever date or be intimate with another woman ever again. Mike, I've asked myself that same question, but right now it's too soon, all the hurt and anger is still new to me, with those feelings ever go away, yes, but it takes time. And I have to think of the girls too don't want to do anything that will cause them to distrust me. When I was in prison Omar, several nights I laid in my bunk thinking about how it must be for you, the only feelings that came to mind was sadness and lost. Mike have you ever been in the dark with the lights off trying to find your way around, that's how I felt for the first year. Your mom would always check up on me and the girls, when she was getting around good by herself. She even helps me out with the girls when Tosha was going back and forth in the hospital. Your mother was a kind lady with a giving spirit, and you remind me of her Mike. When my parents were killed in the car accident, it was your mom who came to my aid. She cared for me like I was her own child. After you went to prison me and Tosha told your mother the whole story about what happen, she just said that she knows one day that something would happen to make a bond between us that can never be broken. When she sat back quiet, and we run the streets. She would tell us always to have each other's backs, who knew it would of came to that. Life or should I say God had his own plan for us, look at you now. Another question Omar, why did you choose to hang around Tony more than me. Because Tony knew what he wanted and how he was going to get it. It hurts me to leave you when I went to college, but I wanted a better life. You were wild and out of control, you turned down a football scholarships and one basketball, Mike you were the man in sports back then, but you wanted the streets more. Never told you this Mike, but I idolized you back then, you were young and talented and had the world at your feet. When you got locked up for that pistol, you went downhill from there. Mama Sarah told me to concentrate more on school and less on these streets, because one day the street game is going to play out. Now Mike let me ask you a question, do you have any regrets. Omar, bro when I first went to prison. Yes, I had regrets because everything that I did landed me there. But after looking at myself in the mirror and realizing that I did this to myself a long time ago. Taking that charge for you didn't send me to prison, it freed me. Bro, I had become a prisoner of these streets, with the drugs, alcohol, and women, I needed to be freed. I hate to say but God knew what he was doing, he doesn't make mistakes like man. Look at me Omar, I mean really look at me, I'm not that same person, you use to know. I'm glad you've change because the old you would of tore Louis head off. Louis is lucky Omar, but eventually his luck is going to run out. Omar does the old neighborhood still look the same. No, Mike they tore down a lot of apartments and replaced them with upscale houses, that no one could afford. The hood is not the hood anymore, you have only a few that's left and didn't sell their land. What about the corner store, you're old hang out Mike is still there? Old man Sam died and left everything to his children. What about Chris, he got shot in the head and died a few days after you turned yourself in the other night after we left the hospital, I wanted to talk to Felicia, but she wasn't answering the phone, so something told me to ride by the park we use to hang out at and there she was. The park doesn't look as big as it was when we were little. Things change Mike, remember when we use to eat green plums off the tree in your cousin's yard, yes, I remember, when was the last time you had one. It's been a while; you don't have a taste for them anymore do you. What are you trying to say Omar? Growing up requires us to leave old habits to enjoy new ones, they can be good for us or cause us more grief in our lives. Changes was coming whether we wanted it or not Omar. As we rode through the old neighborhood, I spotted Chris little sister Mya all grown up now. When me and Omar pulled over to talk to her, at first, she didn't recognize us, but as we talked, she started to remember that I was the guy that her brother hung out with all the time. Yes, she said Mike Johnson, my brother Chris dude died. What happen to you Mike you just up and disappeared on everybody. Mya, I went to prison for seven years didn't

Chris tell you. No Mike after you stop coming around my brother started smoking lace blunts with his girlfriend and went down here from there. He got involved in robbing people and one day he robbed the wrong person, and that same person found my brother and killed him. Sorry to hear that Mya, so how you've been doing and how's your mother. I'm doing okay, working and paying my way through school, mom's doing good too, just taking life as it comes. Here's my number Mya, if you and your mom need anything, give me a call. Your mom still stays in the same house. Yes Mike. Okay and we said goodbye. Omar looked at me saying, that could have been one of us Mike. Seems like she's headed in the right direction. I'm going to check in on her Omar, these streets haven't gotten to her yet, helping her out with school may just help her out. We all need a little help sometimes, if its only word of encouragement. We decided to stop by old man Sam's store, but it was boarded up with a for sale sign in front of it. After cruising around we finally made it to my mom's house. Felicia told me that everything was left the way it was, and no one has been in the house since my mom passing away. Looking over at Omar hesitating to get out the car Omar asked me are you ready to do this Mike, I know that it's hard, but this has to be done now or later. We all need closure sometimes on certain puts of our life especially death. I replied let's do this and get this over with. Using my old key I opened the front door, house smelling the same as when I was a kid walking into that house was like rewinding back time. Entering the living room and seeing all the old pictures of me as a child and until now. Seeing the first picture me and Omar took, my mom had somehow gotten it and frame it. Me and Omar laughing at the outfits we had on and the way that our hair was cut. Then there it was, the only picture my mom had of my dad, sitting in a chair smiling pointing at the camera. That's when the emotions hit me, finally coming to terms that I miss them so much. Been trying to keep myself busy so that I wouldn't have to think about it. But today is the day to settle this. The little time that I did get a chance to spend with my dad was a blessing. He always instilled in me life is what you make it. To this day I can still hear those words being said to me. Trying not to remember that day at the age of ten walking into a crowded house and seeing my mom in tears, saying to me someone had shot my dad. Sometimes I wonder, was that time cause to make me take to the streets like I did. One reason why I put off coming to this house was because of the painful memories. Don't get me wrong we did have a few good ones. But not as many as the bad ones. Omar coming to stay with us bring some much-needed light to a dim and dark place. As I continue to walk around the house everything seems to be in place like somebody had been living in the house. Finally making my way to my old room and laying in my bed asleep was my cousin Felicia. Tapping her on the shoulder trying to wake her up, she looked at me still half-asleep saying, I knew the two of you would show up soon. Not knowing what to say, I just let her do the talking. Ever since I left Louis I've been staying here not wanting to go back to my place, didn't want to run into Louis or Nicole. She's been calling my phone, throwing in my face that she has Louis now. Mike and Omar, I'm four months pregnant with Louis child and I haven't got a clue about what to do. Mike you're the only family I've got, please help me. Before I could response Omar grabbed Felicia and hugged her telling her I'm your family too we'll get through this together, Mama Sarah would want that. All the memories of my mom's house didn't seem to bother me anymore, the old memories seemed to be passing away and the start of new ones. Right then my question had been answer about the house, Felicia was going to stay in it her and the baby.

Louis

Ever since Nicole showed up at the hospital claiming that she was sorry for what she did we've been together. Haven't spoken to the guys because I'm really not in the mood for a lecture from neither of them. Nicole explained to me how her emotion gotten the best of her. At first, I didn't really know what to do when she shows up at the hospital unexpected crying. For her to have the guts to show up at the hospital knowing how I probable felt made me wonder at her intentions. So, I sat and listen to what she had to say, and she somehow talked me into letting her take care of me. As we left the hospital my guard was still up because what she had just did to me was fresh on my mind. She didn't take me to her house, but instead drive all the way to her mom's house in Savannah. When I asked Nicole why she wanted to take me to her mom's she answered so she can take care of me without any interruptions, that she knew Omar and the guys would be at my house. After a couple of days of her waiting on my hand and foot, I started sleeping back with her without a condom. Every time we had sex, she wanted me to come inside of her, at first, I wanted to get her pregnant myself, but as I started thinking, was all this put of her plan again. Plan or no plan she got what she wanted, Nicole's three months pregnant after she got pregnant and we went to the doctor, we both decided to put the past behind us and look to the future. I was finally starting a family and couldn't share the news with my brothers because of my actions. Tony the one I thought would be on my side but after disappearing and not answering their phone calls, they had washed their hands with me. At this point I really didn't care what they thought. me and Nicole was happy together but in some odd way, I still wasn't satisfied. Nicole sexually satisfied me, but it was something deeper than that. Maybe as our relationship grow that feeling will go away. After staying a couple of months at her mom's house we finally came back to my place. All the old spots me and the guys hung out at I avoided, wasn't really ready for their disapproval of me being with Nicole. I often thought of Felicia, how's she's doing. Who she's with, and where she's at and then I come back to reality and think about how I just fucked over her? Didn't mean for things to go the way they did. Felicia treated me like a king, regardless of how I may have treated her in the past, she always had my back. When I did in months in jail for possession of cocaine, she never missed a visit, accepted all of my phone calls and always kept money on my books. Felicia was good to me, a little too good that I took advantage of. I wonder will she ever talk to me again and then there's Mike, the guy that taught me everything, when I was in a jail, Mike would come bail me out, and I played his favorite cousin like that. One day I'll have to face them and who can guess what's going to happen. While my stay in Savannah, they fired me from the Kia plant, just had made supervisor. No money coming in I had to go back to the streets. My brothers weren't talking to me so I just couldn't go to them and get a loan until another job come through for me. Nicole hooked me up with some people she knew. Nicole still had her job as a flight attendant, but eventually she would have to take a leave of absence until she has the baby. Going back to the streets wasn't hard for me, all of my homeboys was still out there slinging packages and doing big boy things. Riding through the neighborhood I spotted my old junkie friend Jeff, asking him a couple of questions about where the hot spots was and then I asked about old man Sam store and he looked at me crazy and said, you haven't heard your boy Mike bought that store two weeks ago. It's under renovation. You tell me that's your boy and you haven't heard, man that's the talk of the town. Jeff I've been out of town for the last few months haven't caught up with him yet. Him and his cousin Felicia been moving stuff out of his mom's house, I think they over there now. I just said OKAY to Jeff and pulled off. So, Mike doing big things in the hood and Felicia's with him. I decided to drive by Mike's mom house and old man Sam's store and there was the both of them standing outside talking to some white guy. I couldn't take my eyes off Felicia for nothing. It was something about her that was different. When I passed by Felicia looked up and seen me driving by. Seeing Felicia again made me second guess myself about being with Nicole. Even though I made the decision to be with Nicole, somehow my feelings were still there with Felicia. Looking in her eyes I could still see the hurt that I caused her but it's something different about her, look like she gained some weight. After running into a couple of more old friends, Nicole called to see where I was and when would I be home. She was coming in from L.A. and wanted me to pick her up at the airport. Later that night on the ride home, Felicia's face kept popping up in my head. I could see now that Mike was keeping his cousin close to him. Ever since Mike been home, he seemed to be making some good business deals. Omar and Tony got to have they hand in it some kind of way. I wonder if I would have stayed in that hospital and waited on the guy's how things would be. My actions had caused a big division between me and my friends, and now they were making moves and deals without me. Never thought that I'll feel alone on these streets. Someway I have to make things right between me and my brothers. First, I've got to man up and talk to Mike, I know that maybe a hard thing to do, but it must be done. When me and Mike use to hustle in the streets together he always told me he wouldn't never let anything, or anyone come between us. Didn't know that things between me and Felicia would be like they were. Nicole was just a chick that I was supposed to have fun with, not to make a relationship with. Things are set in motion now and there's no turning back. Waiting around my house waiting on Nicole to call I decide to try and call Mike. Every time I called the voicemail picked up. After the three call I finally built my nerves up to leave a message. Felicia had my emotions all over the place. A part of me wanted to get on my knees and crawl back to her, but that not going to work. Something more would have to be done before I would even try to talk to her. Well since Mike don't want to answer the phone, maybe it was time I made special visit to his house, but first I was going to talk Omar into going with me.

Tony and Michelle

After spending these last few weeks with Michelle and Keisha, I decided to take them to meet my parents in Florida. Ever since my graduation from college, they just up and moved to Florida. They are retired General Motors workers and they both wanted a change of scenery. Michelle meets my parents once before in my first year of college. She was introduced as a good friend then, but things have changed a lot since then. We all have been getting along good, it was a little strange to all of us at first, but once we started getting to know each other all over again, things begin to go smoothly than. Michelle wanted me to drive instead of catching a plane, that way we could spend more time together. Keisha enjoyed the ride; this was her first-time leaving, Georgia. Seeing the palms, and peach tree up close was amazing to her, but what caught her eyes was the big sandy beaches. We planned to stay at my parent's beach house instead of a hotel. Haven't seen my parents in a year, but I check in with them a few times a week to let them know how I'm doing my mom always asked me when I was going to settle down and have kids, she wanted to spend some time with a grandchild before she died. Me being the only child. On the phone I told them both, that I had a surprise for them. Unlike a few of the guys, both my parents raised me Omar use to come and spend weekends at the house. But the one my parents were crazy about and had high expectation of was Mike. Man, dad never missed Mike's basketball or football games. When Mike chooses the streets over school my dad washed his hands with Mike. When Mike went to prison it devastated my dad to the point that he almost had a heart attack. After a few years in prison, Mike begins writing letters to my dad and eventually my dad visited him. My dad and

Mike have they own relationship with each other, that they both never talk about. Mike shocked me the other day, when he called me to help him and Omar to purchase old man Sam's store. He's really making moves to build him a future for him and Tiffany. I'm really glad for them both. When I finally pulled into the driveway of my parent's beach home, for the first time in my life. I wasn't rushing to do anything but taking things slow and enjoying every minute. Looking at Michelle and Keisha, smiling at me, without no worries looks in their eyes. Could this be the life that God plan for me all along. When we got out of the car, my mom opened the door with a smile on her face but with a puzzled look. Before I could say anything, who is this pretty little girl and pretty lady you have with you Tony, my mom asked. This is the surprise I was telling you I had for you. Mom meet Keisha my daughter and Michelle my fiancée. Never thought I'll be saying that so soon, but it sounded and felt good. Mom pushed me to the side and touched Keisha's face, after looking her over, my mom looked at me and pulled Keisha to her and begin to cry. While she was hugging Keisha with one arm she reached out to Michelle with the other arm and pulled her close for a hug too. My mom was crying so loud that my dad came running from the living room to see what was wrong with my mom. When my mom introduced Keisha and Michelle to him, he couldn't say anything he just looked at both of them and pulled up a seat and sat down. Trying to pull Keisha away from my mom was impossible for my dad, she wouldn't let Keisha go we all sat down at the kitchen table. When did all this happen son, my dad asked? I looked at Michelle and said do you want to tell or me, she answered you. So, I explained to my parents everything that had went down between me and Michelle, not leaving nothing out. My dad looked over at Michelle and told her that she could of came to them for help. But Michelle explains how she ran back to her family and didn't want to bother anybody about her pregnancy. No more questions my mom said cutting in on my dad. Today is a new day for this family, Michelle did what she had to do as a mother. What is your name little girl my dad asked, Keisha Michelle Robinson she answered my dad? So, you're a Robinson, yes, I am Keisha said with a shy girlish grin. Have you ever seen the beach up close Keisha's dad asked, no this is my first-time sir? Please don't call me sir, call me papa. Okay she responded. Tony let's take Keisha out on the deck so she can get a better view of the beach while

Michelle and your mother talk. Michelle smiled at me as me, my dad and Keisha headed out on the deck. I couldn't begin to imagine what my mom and Michelle was going to talk about. I can remember back at my first time really to enjoy the beach at an early age. Couldn't believe all this water in one place. Keisha just stared out at all the water and then asked my dad when will he take her swimming. Before he answered Keisha, he looked at me and asked, how long did we plan on staying, just a few days, dad, I wanted you and mom to get to know Keisha and Michelle I explain to him. Then he turns to Keisha, do you have a swimming suit with you, yes papa, me and dad went shopping the other night and got me one. As my dad was getting to know his granddaughter, I took a glace into the kitchen and Michelle and my mom was laughing and talking like old friends. Spending the next two days with my parent is turning out easier than I thought. That night after all getting to know each other for the first time was over me and my dad finally had a chance to talk. Tony my son, you're finally on the right path. To tell you the truth, the way you were going, never thought you would settle down, after you told me about that girl breaking your heart. Then my dad stops in midsentence, she's the one isn't she he asked. He continued to talk, asking all kinds of questions until he got his nerves up to ask, is she the one Tony you plan on marrying. That same question had been asked by Omar and Mike and me. Yes, she is dad, as soon as we get back to Atlanta, I'm going to ask her. Why wait do it now son, I haven't gotten the ring yet dad. As soon as that came out of my mouth, Michelle walked into the room smiling and asking what we're talking about. My dad told her she was the main topic of the conversation. And then my dad did the unusually, he asked Michelle what her plans for me and her. At first, she had this shock look on her face and then she smiled and answered, I plan on spending the rest of my life with him. With that reply my dad hugged Michelle and told both of us goodnight. Today has been a long day for the three of us, I said to Michelle. I'm really enjoying myself Tony, didn't think it would be like this. Your mom was so nice to me and Keisha. She told me no matter what, that me and Keisha is always welcome at her house. Michelle took my hands into hers, kissed me on my lips and said Tony I really want this for us, I've never seen Keisha so happy, we both need you. At that moment I felt a feeling I never had before, it caused me to turn my face from Michelle's. Trying to hold back a tear from rolling down my face, nobody has ever said that to me Michelle like that. She smiled telling me it's a lot of things she's going to tell me no one else has said to me. Telling me also that's she's just beginning to show me her love, that it's gets better and better. Now I was the one smiling and speechless. I couldn't hold it in anymore, right then I got down on one knee and asked Michelle to marry me, she grabbed my face kissed me and said yes yes yes!!!

Tiffany's Surprise for Mike

For the last couple of weeks, I've been feeling sick. Today was one of the worst days so I decided to go to my doctor while Mike was with Omar and Tony closing the deal on old man Sam's store. Those months are going by fast and soon my wedding day will be here. I called my mom to meet me at the doctor's office. After running all kinds of test on me and when the results came back, I wasn't shocked at all, I was pregnant. My period was three weeks late, so Mike going to be a dad. When my mom heard, she was so happy for us. Maybe the big wedding has to wait because I want to be married before this baby comes. After leaving the doctor's office, I stop by the mall to pick up a few things to make this a night to remember for Mike. Walking through the malls looking for the right pieces to my dream night and run into someone I didn't want to see Louis. Louis didn't look like the same person I was introduce to some months back. He'd lost weight and looked very worried. Mike hadn't talk to Louis since he left the hospital with Nicole. He approached me with his head down, not trying to look me in my face. Hi, Tiffany I know I'm the last person on earth you want to talk to, but please just give me a minute of your time Louis asked in a humble voice. I agreed and we walked over to the food court to sit down. He still wouldn't look me in my eyes and that was really strange of Louis. How's Mike and the guys he asked, I must be really on their shit. List, they won't accept none of my phone calls or return any as while. Tiffany, I know that my actions was wrong towards Felicia, and I regret that every day. Not a day goes by that I don't think about all the pain I caused her. A couple of weeks ago I was riding through the old neighborhood and seen her and Mike standing in front of old man Sam's store. I'm so glad to see everything working out for Mike, and he deserves every bit of it.

I'm not going to take up too much of your time Tiffany, just like Mike know that I'm truly sorry for all the pain and disrespect, I caused to him and his family. A lot has happened since that day, me leaving the hospital the way I did was dead wrong. Take a good look at me Tiffany, I feel like I'm losing my mind without my best friend. When you talk to him again tell him and the guys that I love them. After he said that without letting me say a word, Louis just got up and left me sitting right there alone. The only thing I could do was to pick up the phone and call Mike. Tears was in my eyes from listening to Louis. Looking at him and his appearance he was really hurt. When Mike answered the phone, I could barely talk, I couldn't even get the words out, I just kept saying Louis name. Mike asked me where I was at. When I told him where I was, he told me to stay there, he would be there in a hot minute, and he hung up. After a few minutes I finally pulled myself together. About ten minutes later Mike and Tony came running through the mall. The only thing I could do was at the time was just to hug Mike. What's wrong Tiff Mike asked, I whispered in his ear, I ran into Louis and his really looking bad. Just seeing him look like that and hearing him apologize over and over. Mike, Louis is really hurting you have to call him, please call him for me. Mike agreed to call Louis, but first he wanted to get me home and calm me down. I asked Mike how did he get here so fast, he told me that he was at Tony's office signing some papers and his office is on the other side of the mall. Then Mike asked me what the doctor said, I told him everything was okay and will talk later about it. Mike and Tony were trying to look through the bags before they put them in the car, but I told both of them to stop being nosey that it was girl stuff, somethings I picked out for my mom. Both of them stop wandering what was in the bags and started back asking questions about Louis. The more I tried to explain to them, I could see the looks of worry on their faces. After a while Mike and I finally got in my car and left. For the first few minutes we were in the car Mike didn't say a word, he just looked out the window with a look of concern for his best friend. Mike touched my shoulder and asked me was he wrong to take Felicia side and just leave his friend in the cold like that. Looking at the expression on Mike's face, this was something that has been bothering him for a while now. Taking a little time to response, Felicia's your family, people always say blood is thicker than water. You made a choice because of the principals you believe now. Baby you made the right decision, you're turning your back on Louis for Felicia, really made Louis look at himself. He's reaching out to you because he feels like, you of all people should understand and forgive him. One day Felicia going to have to tell him that's she carrying his child Mike. So why not call Louis up and talk to him, see what's really going on with him, I'm not taking sides but he's still your friend. You can downplay it all you want you miss him too. Tiffany maybe your right, but it's going to take time. Louis took our trust and friendship for granted, he chooses a female he barely knows over us, friends who have always had his back no matter what. I'll call Louis and talk with him. After I drop Mike off to get his car from Tony's house, he told me he was going to check on Felicia and then come home, that would give me just enough time to get things together my little surprise for Mike tonight. When I talk to my mom at the doctor's office, I told her that the wedding plans was going to be cancelled because soon as Mike hear I'm pregnant he's going to want to marry me right away. She said that that's what she loves about Mike a man with values and said that she wanted to go to the courthouse with us. Every morning for the last month, I've awakened to breakfast in bed with fresh fruit and a single red rose in a wine glass. When I ask Mike what's the occasion, he simply says because every day is a blessing from God to wake up beside you. I've never gazed into a man eye and felt warmness all over my body. My mom told me a long time ago when I was a teenager in love for the first time, when that special one comes in your life, every feeling inside of you will be touch. Never know what she was talking about until now. Having his baby is what I wanted also, maybe more than Mike. Growing up both of my parents was there together. They showed me the love that two people can share through the years no matter what. Most people dream about and want the kind of man I have, right now I'm just thankful that God put him in my life. Tears of joy started running down my face when I pulled into the driveway. Rushing into the house thinking Mike wouldn't be home until later, he pulls into the driveway. Coming in the house smiling carrying teddy bears balloons and flowers. Tiffany, he said, you can't pull nothing over on me, we're pregnant, Mike said. Yes, and how did you know Mike, did my mom call you, no your mom didn't call, your body been telling me every time we make love. You just don't go to the mall in the middle of the week, unless something special has happen. Remember me telling you that I'll never take a moment with you for grant, I pay attention to your every movement every emotion you have I feel, we have truly become one and tomorrow you will become Mrs. Tiffany Johnson my wife.

Omar and the Girls

Lately I've been thinking, will me raising the girls alone will be enough for them. Every morning when I enter their room to wake them up for school is something I look forward too. The girls are my life and if I would lose one of them, I couldn't live with myself. So, every day I try to be better than I was the day before. One thing I've learn over the years is cherish each day, because when that day is gone, it can't be relived. As I look into Diamond's eyes, I see the eagerness that was in her mom. The older she gets the more she reminds of Tosha. Diamond looks at her mom pictures sometimes and ask me, was my mom pretty on the inside too, and my answer to her is that she was beautiful on the inside. Everyday Diamond is starting to ask more and more question about her mom, eventually I knew that it would happen as she got older. Shamekia on the other hand is totally different. Being a teenager, she's coming into her own. I've learned to sit back and watch and not so quick to response to some of her mess ups, but give her the chance to understand what she done and to learn from it. Shamekia has her mom loving spirit, always trying to help someone. Now that's Mike's home, the girls enjoy spending time with him and Tiffany. They somehow understand why Mike so serious about everything. Mike has cancelled the wedding until after the baby is born, but we're all meeting they today after they leave the courthouse. With Tiffany being pregnant Mike couldn't let another day pass without Tiffany being his wife. The girls are excited because they really like Tiffany. Lately when they can't get in touch with Mike, Tiffany always comes in his place. Their spending time with her doing girl stuff gives me a little time to catch oup on things I've been putting off. Everything is still the same way since Tosha died. Her clothes are still hanging up in the closet next to mines. Today is the day to do some changes around the house. Looking at some of the clothes bring back memories of the dates we went on and the outfit she wore. The red dress she had on the night she told me she was pregnant with Shamekia and how happy I was. I knew that removing Tosha's things from the house was going to be hard for me. The family pictures on the wall were a constant reminder of her. The talks that I've been having lately with the girls, was me letting them know that I wasn't forgetting about their mom, that it was just time for me to try and move on from that part of my life. I explained to them both that every time I look at them, I'll see Tosha and that's part of her will never die. Instead of things getting easier for me, each day begin to get a little harder. Seeing my friends starting families with them soon to be wives made me feel a little jealous. Through the years I denied myself the thought of being with anyone else, but lately I've been feeling different after seeing the girls enjoying themselves around Tiffany. Maybe it's time for me to find someone to spend time with. I haven't talk to the girls or my daughters yet because I haven't really made my mind up yet. Through the years girls I use to date before Tosha, I've run into ladies in different places with the hi are you doing and how's life treating you. I never talked about my private life to none of them, but I'm sure they've heard what happen. Slowly I begin putting Tosha things into boxes, certain things of her's bring out different emotions. My mom and father never told me or Mrs. Sarah that a man is suppose to cry. Nothing could prepare me for this, the pain, the sorrow, loneliness and most off all helplessness that the only thing I could do was watch my wife die. So deep into my thoughts never even heard the girls return with Mike and Tiffany, looking up from the boxes, there they were standing in the doorway of my bedroom just staring at me. What are you doing dad Shamekia asked? Trying to pull myself back together before answering her. Doing something I've been putting off for years, picking up your mother's things, and to my surprise, she asked can we help. The tears I couldn't hold back any longer. Yes, you can help me because I'm having a hard time doing it all alone. Diamond came from around Mike and said we're never forget mom dad but it's hard waking up and looking at all her pictures, maybe this will make things easy for us. I was surprised again by my daughter's. So, we are begin packing Tosha's things in boxes, Mike order pizza and wings and it didn't seem so hard then. The girls were asking questions about what we should keep and give away. We kept the wedding dress because one day one of the girls would be married in it. The jewelry was put in the safe. After we finish packing, we all just sat around talking about old times and the girls just laughed at some of the things we did. As it begins to get late Shamekia tapped Mike on the shoulder asking him, what time do ya'll have to be at the courthouse in the morning with packing up Tosha's things, everybody forgot about how late it was. Mike responds back to Shamekia we'll make it on time. The conversation was all about what was being at the courthouse tomorrow. The plan was that we all meet at the courthouse after they get marry, Mike was going to call the guys up and invite them to celebrate at the club he had rented for a small gathering. I come to realize that I'm doing a good job with the girls. They don't know it but they're teaching me a thing or two. Mike had asked for me and the girls to be present. While the girls and Tiffany was still packing, I pulled Mike to the side by ourselves because I really wanted to know was my friend ready for marriage. I looked at Mike like a true friend and a real brother. He did something for me that only a brother would do for another brother, and he never complained about it. Looking at Mike's as he watched Tiffany with the girls, I didn't have to ask was he ready for marriage, just ask him to take his last drink being a single man. He just laughed and hugged me.

(Tiffany and Mike Day)

It was an early morning on May 20th when I realize, I was marrying the woman of my dreams. Staring at her while she was sleeping, made me respect more, everything and everybody that was in my life. The route that I took to get to this place in my life was worth it. Tiffany carried my seed inside of her that wasn't made out of lust or a mistake, it was made from pure love between woman and man. After today, it's not just about me anymore, but us. God knows what he is doing, and he doesn't make any mistakes. The people that's in my life, some have changed, and some are the same, but at the end of the day they still my people. While I was in prison, I had a lot of time to think, about what I was going to do when I was release. I really didn't have a laid-out map, I just sat back and let God drive. Sometimes we let our own desires and wants to get in the way of what's lay out for us. I've seen guys on fire for God and something simple as not getting a visit or not getting money on their books made them forgot everything that God has showed them. Don't get me wrong it can happen to anybody, but if your truly rooted in the word you'll survive the let downs and rough times. We're still humans and we still have a lot to learn, and we battle against things we can't see, but we're trying to figure out and understand through spiritual eyes. Being kissed on my neck by Tiffany saying good morning, brought me out of my deep thinking. The smile of happiness on her face, sent chills all over my body. Never know that I could be a good man to any woman, but things change, people change as well as circumstances. Tiffany jumped up out of the bed saying, I can't believe that we're going to be married to each other in a few hours. I thought that this day would never come for me, but you come into my life and was everything and even more what I wanted in a man. My friends have told me about guys they've dated, while they were locked up, saying they going to do this and that when they get out, but end up doing the same thing that got them there in the first place, but you didn't do nothing to get in there. When Tosha told me the whole story behind what happen, I knew then, that you were a different kind of guy. She said that you didn't never ask for anything or threatening anybody to do stuff for you. That even made me want to get to know you even more, so I waited and prayed on that phone call from you. When you gave me a chance to come see you, that look in your eyes and the conversation in that prison visitation room had me feeling all type of ways. That's why I got me a hotel in that little country town and was the first visitor there that Sunday morning. That night and every other night since then, I counted down the days until you come home. Mike, I fell in love with you that first prison visit. If you asked me to marry you back then, I would have said yes. You've been the only man that I kept myself for. Haven't talked to a man ever since you called me from jail. Never felt like this before and it scares me sometimes because, I don't know how I would act if you ever left me. Tears begin to roll down her eyes, looking at her cry made me cry. I jumped off the bed hugged her and whispered in her ear; I'll never leave you beautiful. Sitting her down on the bed I pulled her face to mines and kissed her softly on her lips. Looking in her eyes I shared something that I had been holding in until this day. I like to lost you our first time trying to date. One night I got on my knees and ask God to give me a second chance with you. I promise to God that I would never mistreat and would love you like he loved the world. Tiffany at night sometimes I just look at you while you're sleeping, admiring your beauty and thanking God at the same time for bringing you back. My prayers were answered and yours too. Today is our day, we're going to enjoy it with family and friends today our life starts as being one in everything we do. If you shine, I shine, if I shine, you shine. We haven't experience hard times or a disagreement, I know they're going to come and we're going to go through some things, but just know I'm not going anywhere, and I promise you that. We kissed each other again and started getting ready to leave. When we arrived at the courthouse, Mike and the girls was waiting along with Tiffany parents. As we walked towards them, I could see the smiles on their face from a distance. Omar hugged me and said, Let's do this bro. The girls crowded around Tiffany hugging each other parents also. So, we all went into the judge's chamber but before the judge was about to marry us, I had a couple of words to say to Tiffany. Seven years ago, I was stranded on a desert island all alone, and in the distance, I seen a small boat coming towards me. It was so far away that I could barely see as it got closer, I woke up out of my dream, for a visitation call. When I walked into that visitation room and I seen you, that dream came back to remembrance. You were that small boat coming to save me off that island. I seen you in my dreams several times before, but I just had to be patience until, me myself was right

The Talk

Don't really have time to do the big honeymoon thing, because of the opening of the store and me and the guys had made plans to talk to Louis. Tiffany wanted to tag along but we wouldn't let her. We met at the bar not too far from the store. Tiffany was right, Louis had lost some weight and the worrying had taken a toll on Louis's face. Tony and Omar were still mad but it's they boy and we're all human and entitled to make bad choices in life. We all sat down at the table and Louis spoke. He explained his actions over the last time we seen him. He spoke about letting the drugs take over his life, thinking that we all were in competition with one another. Everything was getting harder and harder every day for him without his friends to talk too. Through the years he always felt that he wasn't living up to the man he supposed to be. Come to find out he had checked his self in rehab and had been clean for a month now. He did some searching about Nicole that she was lying about the baby was his. He said that he was sorry about just walking out on us like he did, but the only thing he was thinking about was getting high. Through all this he learned that no matter how good something sounds and looks can be an illusion. After seeing things clearly, he knew he needed to talk to the guys and straighten everything out. Mike was the first one to say something. Louis we're glad that you were man enough to correct and address this matter. We've all made mistakes before and can't nobody sitting at this table can tell me everything different. We all have had some growing up to do so we can't judge you, but you're our boy and yes what you did was really fucked up. But we're all men here and we hear you. You really let us down but the love all of us have for you, we can move on from any disagreements. We been knowing each other forever and we can put this behind us. I'm glad you're getting yourself together and making moves to get control of your life back. It takes a real man to realize he was wrong. For a minute everyone just sat there quite until Omar told Louis that everything sounds good what you're saying but do you really mean that what you're saying. We all forgive you this time but what about the next time Louis. We're all boys true but we have to draw the line somewhere. I never thought that a female would come between us. A month ago, I had to do the second hardest thing in my life, the first one was seeing my wife die so young. I packed up everything in my house that I didn't have the strength to do before. If it wasn't for the bond that all of us have together, I would have never made it. I love you Louis and I forgave you a long time ago because you're my brother and always will be and never forget that. Tony really didn't have nothing to say but glad you getting it together now let's drink not you Louis, stay clean I'll drink enough for both of us laughing. We all sat at the bar eating and drinking like old friends and out the blue Nicole walked up to Louis pulled out a gun and shot Louis in his head point blank, before we could do anything the bartender pulled a gun out and shot Nicole in the chest. Omar was the first one to grab Louis, staying hold on hold bro. Tony was sitting there in disbelief on seeing what just happen in front of him. Mike was on the phone calling the ambulance, but

Louis was already gone. Why has this happened to Louis? When the police arrived, Tony had went into shock and had to be rushed to the hospital.

Putting Louis to Rest (Mike)

Still in disbelief I'm burying my brother today. Riding in this family car thinking we never had a chance to tell Louis about Tiffany being pregnant with his child. Thinking back over the years about the good times. I can remember in high school cutting class to ride around with Omar, we always had to wait on Louis. He always was the last one to sneak out the classroom. Laughing because he used to be the one that would get caught sometimes, well most of the time. The day Nicole shot Louis still plays clearly in my mind like it just happens. In life sometimes things aren't meant to bring you pain but wakes you up to let you know nothing is promise in life. Always thought that I would be the first one to go because I was considered the wild one out the bunch. When I went to prison something changed inside of me, it's unexplainable. Things that you use to love to do you hate now. Chasing all kind of women and just do something you know was wrong. People always say if I knew what I know things would be different, but if you knew but then you would of missed out on the good times now. We live in a world that has no love for you. If you can't find inner peace within yourself, how can you feel alive. Looking over at Tiffany takes some of the pain away, and I glance over at Felicia carrying Louis child, my nephew, my brother son.

Omar

Hands are trembling and shaking, bringing back memories that I've tried to bury over the years. Louis didn't deserve to be killed like this, all because he tried to turn his life around and try to be a better person. People just don't know losing someone close to them takes a toll on you. Revisiting the graveyard is never a good thing. We found out from the rehab place, that Nicole had come to the place where Louis was at showing out and said that if she can't have him no one will. He had a restraining order filed against her. Louis was talking to kids trying to tell what he went through and telling them not to go down that path. He had joined the church and was really changing. God knew what he was doing, he gave us one last time to enjoy the new Louis one last time. Maybe Louis seen something we didn't, because all he kept saying I love you guys no matter what yall are my brothers without yall I'm nothing. Now, I still have to be strong because my girls Diamond and Shamekia loved Louis. They keep asking Mike why God keep taking people they love away from them.

Tony

Trying to hold my sanity holding on to Michelle and Keisha's hand tight as I could. God gave me a second chance with Michelle, and nothing is going to change that. Wish Louis could have gotten a second chance to make things right with the people he loved. Looking around the room at my boys seems like a bad dream. Louis was always his own man and he walked to the beat of his own drum. I can remember the good days with him, always cracking slick jokes, making our days a little easier. I hate he's not going to be here to be around seeing Keisha grow up. Louis passing made me take life more serious than I did before. Me, Mike and Omar have to be strong, because we still have a lot of people looking at us. But the people that's looking in from the outside will never understand what we've been through. We always have had our ups and downs like friends will always have, but a higher power and the love and respect we had for each other always kept us close. I know that it's going to be hard on Mike's sister. Can't begin to comprehend or imagine what she's going through. She has to raise a baby without a father, but she has three of us for the rest of the baby's life.

New Beginnings

This last year has been rough on all three of us. Losing Louis like we did to make us second guess ourselves turning our backs on him for that short period of time. We visit his grave site at least once a month, just to talk like we use to. My sister Felicia had a son and we named him Louis Jr. She's still grieving, but eventually that we passed for all of us. It's not easy losing a close friend but like the pastor said at the funeral, life goes on and old wounds would heal, and the pain will go away, but memories will last forever. The conversations we use to have will never be forgotten. Every time I see my nephew I see my friend Louis. Nicole survives and is doing life in prison and come to find out the baby really was Louis. I visited her at the jail and me being a God-filled man, I felt her pain. She herself didn't know who the baby was, but we she finally had proof that it was Louis he was nowhere to be found. Evidently she heard about Louis going to the rehab where she showed out on him, and he put the restraining on her. After that day she hated Louis and wanted him dead because she thought it was all a scram. That's something we'll never know. She's had ask Tony and Michelle to adopted the pretty little girl. I see now, when we say we have things planned out for our lives God laughs, because God already has plans for us. Tony and Michelle are getting married in a couple of months. Keisha is with Tony everywhere he goes. Every day she looks more and more like her dad. Michelle sold her house and they moved in with Tony. Tony never thought in a million years that he would be marrying the woman that broke his heart back in the day. He travels to Florida a lot now and his mom and dad comes to visit too. Somethings in life you can't put a time limit on it especially family. You may have your disagreements and fallouts but family still family. Omar went on his first real date, the girls had to give him a couple of pointers on what not to do. It hasn't been easy for Omar. Louis death bring back a lot of feelings Omar has tried to bury over the years. Tosha will always be the love of his life, but he felt like, he needed to move on for the girl's sake. The girls have been spending a lot of time with me and Tiffany helping out with the baby, Diamond and Shamekia is going up and all that you see in them is their mom. The girls know that no one will ever take the place of their mom. They just wanted their dad to feel normal and be happy again. I just want to wish my buddy the best in life because I'll do it all over again for him. We'll Tiffany blessed me with a son, yes, he's a junior, I wouldn't have it no other way. It took us some time to get where we're at but we're here now and enjoying every minute. All the trials and tribulations I had to go through, wouldn't change it for the world. The prison sentence, the long days not knowing was I going to make it out alive, no complaints because looking at the man I'm now. The Bible says when I was a child I though as a child but when I put childish things away, became a man. Tiffany is a good thing for me, and I plan on loving her for the rest of my life. One thing I can say is I love the conversation of men.

Printed in the United States
by Baker & Taylor Publisher Services